In the Year 2889
and Other
Science Fiction
Stories

In the Year 2889 and Other Science Fiction Stories

Vitasta

Published by
Vitasta Publishing Pvt Ltd
4348/4C, Ansari Road, Daryaganj
New Delhi - 110 002
info@vitastapublishing.com

ISBN: 978-81-19670-06-2

First Edition 2025
MRP ₹350

We gratefully acknowledge Project Gutenberg and Internet Archive for making this book possible.

Compiled and Edited by Abhishek Rana
Typeset & Cover Design by Rohit Gautam
Printed by Vikas Computer and Printers, New Delhi

Contents

Publisher's Note

This collection brings together eleven groundbreaking stories from the pioneers of science fiction.

Written in an age of rapid scientific progress, these stories reflect both the excitement and anxiety of their times. The authors dared to ask 'what if?' long before many of their imagined technologies became reality. Here you'll find Jules and Michel Verne's predictions of future inventions, Hawthorne's explorations of human nature through science, and Poe's blend of logic and terror.

We've carefully preserved the original texts while making them accessible to modern readers. Each story serves as a window into how past generations viewed the promise and peril of scientific advancement. Whether you're new to these classics or revisiting old favorites, we hope these timeless tales will spark your imagination.

Jerome K Jerome

(1859-1927)

A British humorist best known for *Three Men in a Boat,* a hilarious account of a boating holiday. He started life poor, worked various jobs including actor and journalist, and became one of England's most popular comic writers.

The New Utopia

Jerome K Jerome

I had spent an extremely interesting evening. I had dined with some very 'advanced' friends of mine at the 'National Socialist Club'. We had had an excellent dinner: the pheasant, stuffed with truffles, was a poem; and when I say that the '49 Chateau Lafitte was worth the price we had to pay for it, I do not see what more I can add in its favour.

After dinner, and over the cigars (I must say they do know how to stock good cigars at the National Socialist Club), we had a very instructive discussion about the coming equality of man and the nationalisation of capital.

I was not able to take much part in the argument myself, because, having been left when a boy in a position which rendered it necessary for me to earn my own living, I have never enjoyed the time and opportunity to study these questions.

But I listened very attentively while my friends explained how, for the thousands of centuries during which it had existed before they came, the world had been going on all wrong, and how, in the course of the next few years or so, they meant to put it right.

Equality of all mankind was their watchword—perfect equality in all things—equality in possessions, and equality in position and influence, and equality in duties, resulting in equality in happiness and contentment.

The world belonged to all alike, and must be equally divided. Each man's labour was the property, not of himself, but of the State which fed and clothed him, and must be applied, not to his own aggrandisement, but to the enrichment of the race.

Individual wealth—the social chain with which the few had bound the many, the bandit's pistol by which a small gang of robbers had thieved—must be taken from the hands that too long had held it.

Social distinctions—the barriers by which the rising tide of humanity had hitherto been fretted and restrained—must be for ever swept aside. The human race must press onward to its destiny (whatever that might be), not as at present, a scattered horde, scrambling, each man for himself, over the broken ground of un-equal birth and fortune—the soft sward reserved for the feet of the pampered, the cruel stones reserved for the feet of the cursed—but an ordered army, marching side by side over the level plain of equity and equality.

The great bosom of our Mother Earth should nourish

all her children, like and like; none should be hungry, none should have too much. The strong man should not grasp more than the weak; the clever should not scheme to seize more than the simple. The earth was man's, and the fulness thereof; and among all mankind it should be portioned out in even shares. All men were equal by the laws of man.

With inequality comes misery, crime, sin, selfishness, arrogance, hypocrisy. In a world in which all men were equal, there would exist no temptation to evil, and our natural nobility would assert itself.

When all men were equal, the world would be Heaven—freed from the degrading despotism of God.

We raised our glasses and drank to EQUALITY, sacred EQUALITY; and then ordered the waiter to bring us Green Char- treuse and more cigars.

I went home very thoughtful. I did not go to sleep for a long while; I lay awake; thinking over this vision of a new world that had been presented to me.

How delightful life would be, if only the scheme of my socialistic friends could be carried out. There would ne no more of this struggling and striving against each other, no more jealousy, no more disappointment, no more fear of poverty! The State would take charge of us from the hour we were born until we died, and provide for all our wants from the cradle to the coffin, both inclusive, and we should need to give no thought even to the matter. There would be no more hard work (three hours' labour a day would be the limit, according to our calculations, that the State would require from each adult citizen, and nobody would be allowed to do more—I should not be allowed to do more)—no poor to pity, no rich to envy—no one to look down upon us, no one for us to look down upon (not quite so pleasant this latter reflection)—all our life ordered and arranged for us—nothing to think about except the glorious destiny (whatever that might be) of Humanity!

Then thought crept away to sport in chaos, and I slept.

When I awoke, I found myself lying under a glass case, in a high, cheerless room. There was a label over my head; I turned and read it. It ran as follows:

> This Man Was Found Asleep In A House In London, After The Great Social Revolution Of 1899. From The Account Given By The Landlady Of The House, It Would Appear That He Had Already, When Discovered, Been Asleep For Over Ten Years (She Having Forgotten To Call Him). It W As Decided, For Scientific Purposes, Not To Awake Him, But Just To See How Long He Would Sleep On, And He Was Accordingly Brought And Deposited In The 'Museum Of Curiosities', On February 11Th, 1900.

Visitors are requested not to squirt water through the air-holes.

An intelligent-looking old gentleman, who had been arranging some stuffed lizards in an adjoining case, came over and took the cover off me.

'What's the matter?' he asked; 'anything disturbed you?'

'No,' I said; 'I always wake up like this, when I feel I've had enough sleep. What century is this?'

'This,' he said, 'is the twenty-ninth century. You have been asleep for just one thousand years.'

'Ah! well, I feel all the better for it,' I replied, getting down off the table. 'There's nothing like having one's sleep out.'

'I take it you are going to do the usual thing.' said the old gentleman to me, as I proceeded to put on my clothes, which had been lying beside me in the case. 'You'll want me to walk round the city with you, and explain all the changes to you, while you ask questions and make silly remarks?'

'Yes,' I replied, 'I suppose that's what I ought to do.'

'I suppose so,' he muttered. 'Come on, and let's get it over,' and he led the way from the room.

As we went downstairs, I said: 'Well, is it all right, now?' 'Is what all right?' he replied.

'Why, the world,' I replied. 'A few friends of mine were arranging, just before I went to bed, to take it to pieces and fix it up again properly. Have they got it all right by this time? Is everybody equal now, and sin and sorrow and all that sort of thing done away with?'

'Oh, yes,' replied my guide; 'you'll find everything all right now. We've been working away pretty hard at things while you've been asleep. We've just got this earth about perfect now, I should say. Nobody is allowed to do anything wrong or silly; and as for equality, tadpoles ain't in it with us.'

(He talked in rather a vulgar manner, I thought; but I did not like to reprove him.)

We walked out into the city. It was every clean and very quiet. The streets, which were designated by numbers, ran out from each other at right angles, and all presented exactly the same appearance. There were no horses or carriages about; all the traffic was conducted by electric cars. All the people that we met wore a quiet grave expression, and were so much like each other as to give one the idea that they were all members of the same family. Everyone was dressed, as was also my guide, in a pair of grey trousers, and a grey tunic, buttoning tight round the neck and fastened round the waist by a belt. Each man was clean shaven, and each man had black hair.

I said:

'Are all men twins?'

'Twins! Good gracious, no!' answered my guide. 'Whatever made you fancy that?'

'Why, they all look so much alike,' I replied; 'and they've all got black hair!'

'Oh; that's the regulation colour for hair,' explained my companion: 'we've all got black hair. If a man's hair is not black naturally, he has to have it dyed black.'

'Why?' I asked.

'Why!' retorted the old gentleman, somewhat irritably. 'Why, I thought you understood that all men were now equal. What would become of our equality if one man or woman were allowed to swagger about in golden hair, while another had to put up with carrots? Men have not only got to be equal in these happy days, but to look it, as far as can be. By causing all men to be clean shaven, and all men and women to have black hair cut the same length, we obviate, to a certain extent, the errors of Nature.'

I said: 'Why black?'

He said he did not know, but that was the colour which had been decided upon.

'Who by?' I asked.

'By THE MAJORITY,' he replied, raising his hat and lowering his eyes, as if in prayer.

We walked further, and passed more men. I said:

'Are there no women in this city?'

'Women!' exclaimed my guide. 'Of course there are. We've passed hundreds of them!'

'I thought I knew a woman when I saw one,' I observed; 'but I can't remember noticing any.'

'Why, there go two, now,' he said, drawing my attention to a couple of persons near to us, both dressed in the regulation grey trousers and tunics.

'How do you know they are women?' I asked.

'Why, you see the metal numbers that everybody wears on their collar?'

'Yes: I was just thinking what a number of policeman you had, and wondering where the other people were!'

'Well, the even numbers are women; the odd numbers are men.'

'How very simple,' I remarked. 'I suppose after a little practice you can tell one sex from the other almost at a glance?'

'Oh yes,' he replied, 'if you want to.' We walked on in silence for a while. And then I said: 'Why does everybody have a number?'

'To distinguish him by,' answered my companion.

'Don't people have names, then?' 'No.' 'Why?'

'Oh! there was so much inequality in names. Some people were called Montmorency, and they looked down on the Smiths; and the Smythes did not like mixing with the Joneses: so, to save further bother, it was decided to abolish names altogether, and to give everybody a number.'

'Did the Montmorencys and the Smythes object.'

'Yes: but the Smiths and Joneses were in THE MAJORITY.'

'And did no the Ones and Twos look down upon the Threes and Fours, and so on?'

'At first, yes. But, with the abolition of wealth,

numbers lost their value, except for industrial purposes and for double acrostics, and now No. 100 does not consider himself in any way superior to No. 1,000,000.'

I had not washed when I got up, there being no conveniences for doing so in the Museum, and I was begining to feel somewhat hot and dirty. I said:

'Can I wash myself anywhere?'

He said: 'No; we are not allowed to wash ourselves. You must wait until half-past four, and then you will be washed for tea.'

'Be washed!' I cried.

'Who by?'

'The State.'

He said that they had found they could not maintain their equality when people were allowed to wash themselves. Some people washed three or four times a day, while others never touched soap and water from one year's end to the other, and in consquence there got to be two distinct classes, the Clean and the Dirty. All the old class prejudices began to be revived. The clean despised the dirty, and the dirty hated the clean. So, to end dissension, the State decided to do the washing itself, and each citizen was now washed twice a day by government–appointed officials; and private washing was prohibited.

I noticed that we passed no houses as we went along, only block after block of huge, barrack-like buildings, all of the same size and shape. Occasionally, at a corner, we came across a smaller building, labelled 'Museum', 'Hospital', 'Debating Hall', 'Bath', 'Gymnasium', 'Acadeny of Sciences', 'Exhibition of Industries', 'School of Talk', etc., etc.; but never a house.

I said: 'Doesn't anybody live in this town?'

He said: 'You do ask silly questions; upon my word, you do. Where do you think they live?'

I said: 'That's just what I've been trying to think. I don't see any houses anywhere!'

He said:

'We don't need houses—not houses such as you are thinking of. We are socialistic now; we live together in fraternity and equality. We live in these blocks that you see. Each block accommodates one thousand citizens. It contains one thousand beds—one hundred in each room—and bath–rooms and dressing–rooms in proportion, a dining–hall and kitchens. At seven o'clock every morning a bell is rung, and ever one rises and tidies up his bed. At seven–thirty they go into the dressing–rooms, and are washed and shaved and have their hair done. At eight o'clock breakfast is served in the dining-hall. It comprises a pint of oatmeal porridge and half–a–pint of warm milk for each adult citizen. We are all strict vegetarians now. The vegetarian vote increased enormously during the last century, and their organisation being very perfect, they have been able to dictate every election for the past fifty years. At one o'clock another bell is rung, and the people return to dinner, which consists of beans and stewed fruits, with rolly–polly pudding twice a week, and plum–duff on Saturdays. At five o'clock there is tea, and at ten the lights are put out and everbody goes to bed. We are all equal, and we all live alike—clerk and scavenger, tinker and apothecary—all together in fraternity and liberty. The men live in blocks on this side of town, and the women are at the other end of the city.'

'Where are the married people kept?' I asked.

'Oh, there are no married couples,' he replied; 'we abolished marriage two hundred years ago. You see, married life did not work at all well with our system. Domestic life, we found, was thoroughly anti–socialistic in its tendencies. Men thought more of their wives and families than they did of the State. They wished to labour for the benefit of their little circle of beloved ones rather than for the good of the community. They cared more for the future of their children than for the Destiny of Humanity. The ties of love and blood bound men together fast in little groups instead of in one great whole. Before considering the advancement of the human race, men considered the advancement of their kith and kin. Before striving for the greatest happiness of the greatest number, men strove for the happiness of the few who were near and dear to them. In secret, men and women hoarded up and laboured and denied themselves, so as, in secret, to give some little extra gift of joy to their beloved. Love stirred the vice of ambition in men's hearts. To win the smiles of the women they loved, to leave a name behind them that their children might be proud to bear, men sought to raise themselves above the general level, to do some deed that should make the world look up to them and honour them above their fellow–men, to press a deeper footprint than another's upon the dusty high–way of the age. The fundamental principles of Socialism were being daily thwarte and contemned. Each house was a revolutionary centre for the propagation of individualism and personality. From the warmth of each domestic hearth grew up the vipers, Comradeship and Independence, to sting the State and poison the minds of men.

'The doctrines of equality were openly disputed. Men, when they loved a woman, thought her superior to every other woman, and hardly took any pains to disguise their opinion. Loving wives believed their husbands to be wiser and braver and better than all other men. Mothers laughed at the idea of their children being in no way superior to other children. Children imbibed the hideous heresy that their father and mother were the best father and mother in the world.

'From whatever point you looked at it, the Family stood forth as our foe. One man had a charming wife and two sweet–tempered children; his neighbour was married to a shrew, and was the father of eleven noisy, ill–dispositioned brats—where was the equality?

'Again, wherever the Family existed, there hovered, ever contending, the angels of Joy and Sorrow; and in a world where joy and sorrow are known, Equality cannot live. One man and woman, in the night, stand weeping beside a little cot. On the other side of the lath–and–plaster, a fair young couple, hand in hand, are laughing at the silly antics of a grace–faced, gurgling baby. What is poor Equality doing?

'Such things could not be allowed. Love, we saw, was our enemy at every turn. He made equality impossible. He brought joy and pain, and peace and suffering in his train. He disturbed men's beliefs, and imperilled the Destiny of Humanity; so we abolished him and all his works.

'Now there are no marriages, and, therefore, no domestic troubles; no wooing, therefore, no heartaching; no loving, therefore no sorrowing; no kisses and no tears.

'We all live together in equality free from the troubling of joy and pain.'

I said: 'It must be very peaceful; but, tell me—I ask the question merely from a scientific standpoint—how do you keep up the supply of men and women?'

He said: 'Oh, that's simple enough. How did you, in your day, keep up the supply of horses and cows? In the spring, so many children, according as the State requires, are arranged for, and carefully bred, under medical supervision. When they are born, they are taken away from their mothers (who, else, might grow to love them), and brought up in the public nurseries and schools until they are fourteen. They are then examined by State-appointed inspectors, who decide what calling they shall be brought up to, and to such calling they are thereupon apprenticed. At twenty they take their rank of citizens, and are entitled to a vote. No difference whatever is made between men and women. Both sexes enjoy equal privileges.'

I said: 'What are the privileges?'

He said: 'Why, all that I've been telling you.'

We wandered on for a few more miles, but passed nothing but street after street of these huge blocks. I said:

'Are there no shops nor stores in this town?'

'No,' he replied.

'What do we want with shops and stores? The State feeds us, clothes us, houses us, doctors us, washes and dresses us, cuts our corns, and buries us. What could we do with shops?'

I began to feel tired with our walk.

I said: 'Can we go in anywhere and have a drink?'

He said: 'A 'drink'! What's a 'drink'? We have half–a–pint of cocoa with our dinner. Do you mean that?'

I did not feel equal to explaining the matter to him, and he evidently would not have understood me if I had; so I said: 'Yes; I meant that.'

We passed a very fine-looking man a little further on, and I noticed that he had one arm. I had noticed two or three rather big-looking men with only one arm in the course of the morning, and it struck me as curious. I remarked about it to my guide.

He said: 'Yes; when a man is much above the average size and strength, we cut one of his legs or arms off, so as to make things more equal; we lop him down a bit, as it were. Nature, you see, is somewhat behind the times; but we do what we can to put her straight.'

I said: 'I suppose you can't abolish her?'

'Well not altogether,' he replied. 'We only wish we could. But,' he added afterwards, with pardonable pride, 'we've done a good deal.'

I said: 'How about an exceptionally clever man. What do you do with him?' 'Well, we are not much troubled in that way now,' he answered. 'We have not come across anything dangerous in the shape of brain–power for some considerable time now. When we do, we perform a surgical operation upon the head, which softens the brain down to the average level.

'I have sometimes thought,' mused the old gentleman,'that it was a pity we could not level up sometimes, instead of always levelling down; but, of course, that is impossible.'

I said: 'Do you think it right of you to cut these people up, and tone them down, in this manner?'

He said: 'Of course, it is right.'

'You seem very cock-sure about the matter,' I retorted. 'Why is it 'of course' right?'

'Because it was done by THE MAJORITY.'

'How does that make it right?' I asked.

'A MAJORITY can do no wrong,' he answered.

'Oh! is that what the people who are lopped off think?'

'They!' he replied, evidently astonished at the question. 'Oh, they are in the minority, you know.'

'Yes; but even the minority has a right to its arms and legs and heads, hasn't it?'

'A minority has NO rights,' he answered.

I said: 'It's just as well to belong to the Majority, if you're thinking of living here, isn't it?'

He said: 'Yes; most of our people do. They seem to think it more convenient.'

I was finding the town somewhat uninteresting, and I asked if we could not go into the country for a change.

My guide said: 'Oh, yes, certainly;' but did not think I should care much for it.

'Oh! but it used to be so beautiful in the country,' I urged, 'before I went to bed. There were great green trees, and grassy, wind–waved meadows, and little rose–decked cottages, and—'

'Oh, we've changed all that,' interrupted the old gentleman; 'it is all one huge market–garden now, divided by roads and canals cut at right angles to each other. There is no beauty in the country now whatever. We have abolished beauty; it interfered with our equality. It was not fair that some people should live among lovely scenery, and other upon barren moors. So we have made it all pretty much alike everywhere now, and no place can lord it over another.'

'Can a man emigrate into any other country?' I asked;' it doesn't matter what country—any other country would do.'

'Oh, yes, if he likes,' replies my companion; 'but why should he? All lands are exactly the same. The whole world is all one people now—one language, one law, one life.'

'Is there no variety, no change anywhere,' I asked.

'What do you do for pleasure, for recreation? Are there any theatres?'

'No,' responded my guide. 'We had to abolish theatres. The histrionic temperament seemd utterly unable to accept the principles of equality. Each actor thought himself the best actor in the world, and superior, in fact, to most other people altogether, I don't know whether it was the same in your day?'

'Exactly the same,' I answered, 'but we did not take any notice of it.'

'Ah! we did,' he replied, 'and, in consequence, shut the theatres up. Besides, our White Ribbon Vigilance Society said that all places of amusement were vicious and degrading; and being an energetic and stout–winded band, they soon won THE MAJORITY over to their views; and so all amusements are prohibited now.'

I said: 'Are you allowed to read books?'

'Well,' he answered, 'there are not many written. You

see, owing to our all living such perfect lives, and there being no wrong, or sorrow, or joy, or hope, or love, or grief in the world, and everything being so regular and proper, there is really nothing much to write about—except, of course, the Destiny of Humanity.'

'True!' I said, 'I see that. But what of the old works, the classics? You had Shakespeare, and Scott, and Thackeray, and there were one or two little things of my own that were not half–bad. What have you done with all those?'

'Oh, we have burned all those old works,' he said. 'They were full of the old, wrong notions of the old wrong, wicked times, when men were merely slaves and beasts of burden.'

He said all the old paintings and sculptures had been likewise destroyed, partly for the same reason, and partly because they were considered improper by the White Ribbon Vigilance Society, which was a great power now; while all new art and literature were forbidden, as such things tended to undermine the principles of equality. They made men think, and the men that thought grew cleverer than those that did not want to think; and those that did not want to think naturally objected to this, and being in THE MAJORITY, objected to some purpose.

He said that, from like considerations, there were no sports or games permitted. Sports and games caused competition, and competition led to inequality.

I said: 'How long do your citizens work each day?'

'Three hours,' he answered; 'after that, all the remainder of the day belongs to ourselves.'

'Ah! that is just what I was coming to,' I remarked.

'Now what do you do with yourselves during those other twenty–one hours?'

'Oh, we rest.'

'What! for the whole twenty–one hours?'

'Well, rest and think and talk.'

'What do you think and talk about?'

'Oh! Oh, about how wretched life must have been in the old times, and about how happy we are, and—and—oh, and the Destiny of Humanity!'

'Don't you ever get sick of the Destiny of Humanity?'

'No, not much.'

'And what do you understand by it? What is the Destiny of Humanity, do you think?'

'Oh!—why to—to go on being like we are now, only more so—everybody more equal, and more things done by electricity, and everybody to have two votes instead of one, and —'

'Thank you. That will do. Is there anything else that you think of? Have you got a religion?'

'Oh, yes.'

'And you worship a God?'

'Oh, yes.'

'What do you call him?'

'THE MAJORITY.'

'One question more—You don't mind my asking you all these questions, by–the–by, do you?'

'Oh, no. This is all part of my three hours' labour for the State.'

'Oh, I'm glad of that. I should not like to feel that I was encroaching on your time for rest; but what I wanted to ask was, do many of the people here commit suicide?'

'No; such a thing never occurs to them.'

I looked at the faces of the men and women that were passing. There was a patient, almost pathetic, expression upon them all. I wondered where I had seen that look before; it seemed familiar to me.

All at once I remembered. It was just the quiet, troubled, wondering expression that I had always noticed upon the faces of the horses and oxen that we used to breed and keep in the old world.

***

Strange! how very dim and indistinct all the faces are around me! And where is my guide? and why am I sitting on the pavement? and—hark! surely that is the voice of Mrs Biggles, my old landlady. Has she been asleep a thousand years, too? She says it is twelve o'clock—only twelve? and I'm not to be washed 'til half–past four; and I do feel so stuffy and hot, and my head is aching. Hulloa! why, I'm in bed! Has it all been a dream? And am I back in the nineteenth century?

Through the open window I hear the rush and roar of old life's battle. Men are fighting, striving, carving out each man his own life with the sword of strength and will. Men are laughing, grieving, loving, doing wrong deeds, doing great deeds,—falling, struggling, helping one another—living!

And I have a good deal more than three hours' work to do today, and I meant to be up at seven; and, oh dear! I do wish I had not smoked so many strong cigars last night!

Ambrose Bierce

(1842-1914)

An American satirist and short story writer known for his cynical wit and dark themes. His most famous works include *The Devil's Dictionary* and *An Occurrence at Owl Creek Bridge*. He mysteriously disappeared in Mexico in 1914 while observing the Mexican Revolution.

The Damned Thing

Ambrose Bierce

I

By the light of a tallow candle, which had been placed on one end of a rough table, a man was reading something written in a book. It was an old account book, greatly worn; and the writing was not, apparently, very legible, for the man sometimes held the page close to the flame of the candle to get a stronger light upon it. The shadow of the book would then throw into obscurity a half of the room, darkening a number of faces and figures; for besides the reader, eight other men were present. Seven of them sat against the rough log walls, silent and motionless, and, the room being small, not very far from the table. By extending an arm any one of them could have touched the eighth man, who lay on the table, face upward, partly covered by a sheet, his arms at his sides. He was dead.

The man with the book was not reading aloud, and no one spoke; all seemed to be waiting for something to occur; the dead man only was without expectation. From the blank darkness outside came in, through the aperture that served for a window, all the ever unfamiliar noises of night in the wilderness—the long, nameless note of a distant coyote; the stilly pulsing thrill of tireless insects in trees; strange cries of night birds, so different from those of the birds of day; the drone of great blundering beetles, and all that mysterious chorus of small sounds that seem always to have been but half heard when they have suddenly ceased, as if conscious of an indiscretion. But nothing of all this was noted in that company; its members were not overmuch addicted to idle interest in matters of no practical importance; that was obvious in every line of their rugged faces—obvious even in the dim light of the single candle. They were evidently men of the vicinity—farmers and woodmen.

The person reading was a trifle different; one would have said of him that he was of the world, worldly, albeit there was that in his attire which attested a certain fellowship with the organisms of his environment. His coat would hardly have passed muster in San Francisco: his footgear was not of urban origin, and the hat that lay by him on the floor (he was the only one uncovered) was such that if one had considered it as an article of mere personal adornment he would have missed its meaning. In countenance the man was rather prepossessing, with just a hint of sternness; though that he may have assumed or cultivated, as appropriate to one in authority. For he was a coroner. It was by virtue of his office that he had possession of the book in which he was reading; it had been found among the dead man's effects—in his cabin, where the inquest was now taking place.

When the coroner had finished reading he put the book into his breast pocket. At that moment the door was pushed open and a young man entered. He, clearly, was not of mountain birth and breeding: he was clad as those who dwell in cities. His clothing was dusty, however, as from travel. He had, in fact, been riding hard to attend the inquest.

The coroner nodded; no one else greeted him.

'We have waited for you,' said the coroner. 'It is necessary to have done with this business to–night.'

The young man smiled. 'I am sorry to have kept you,' he said. 'I went away, not to evade your summons, but to post to my newspaper an account of what I suppose I am called back to relate.'

The coroner smiled.

'The account that you posted to your newspaper,' he said, 'differs probably from that which you will give here under oath.'

'That,' replied the other, rather hotly and with a visible flush, 'is as you choose. I used manifold paper and have a copy of what I sent. It was not written as news, for it is incredible, but as fiction. It may go as a part of my testimony under oath.'

'But you say it is incredible.'

'That is nothing to you, sir, if I also swear that it is true.'

The coroner was apparently not greatly affected by the young man's manifest resentment. He was silent for some moments, his eyes upon the floor. The men about the sides of the cabin talked in whispers, but seldom withdrew their gaze from the face of the corpse. Presently the coroner lifted his eyes and said: 'We will resume the inquest.'

The men removed their hats. The witness was sworn.

'What is your name?' the coroner asked.

'William Harker.'

'Age?'

'Twenty–seven.'

'You knew the deceased, Hugh Morgan?'

'Yes.'

'You were with him when he died?'

'Near him.'

'How did that happen—your presence, I mean?'

'I was visiting him at this place to shoot and fish. A part of my purpose, however, was to study him, and his odd, solitary way of life. He seemed a good model for a character in fiction. I sometimes write stories.'

'I sometimes read them.'

'Thank you.'

'Stories in general—not yours.'

Some of the jurors laughed. Against a sombre background humor shows high lights. Soldiers in the intervals of battle laugh easily, and a jest in the death chamber conquers by surprise.

'Relate the circumstances of this man's death,' said the coroner. 'You may use any notes or memoranda that you please.'

The witness understood. Pulling a manuscript from his breast pocket he held it near the candle, and turning the leaves until he found the passage that he wanted, began to read.

II

'...The sun had hardly risen when we left the house. We were looking for quail, each with a shotgun, but we had only one dog. Morgan said that our best ground was beyond a certain ridge that he pointed out, and we crossed it by a trail through the chaparral. On the other side was comparatively level ground, thickly covered with wild oats. As we emerged from the chaparral, Morgan was but a few yards in advance. Suddenly, we heard, at a little distance to our right, and partly in front, a noise as of some animal thrashing about in the bushes, which we could see were violently agitated.

'We've started a deer,' said. 'I wish we had brought a rifle.'

'Morgan, who had stopped and was intently watching the agitated chaparral, said nothing, but had cocked both barrels of his gun, and was holding it in readiness to aim. I thought him a trifle excited, which surprised me, for he had a reputation for exceptional coolness, even in moments of sudden and imminent peril.

'O, come!' I said. 'You are not going to fill up a deer with quail–shot, are you?'

'Still he did not reply; but, catching a sight of his face as he turned it slightly toward me, I was struck by the pallor of it. Then I understood that we had serious business on hand, and my first conjecture was that we had 'jumped' a grizzly. I advanced to Morgan's side, cocking my piece as I moved.

'The bushes were now quiet, and the sounds had ceased, but Morgan was as attentive to the place as before.

'What is it? What the devil is it?' I asked.

'That Damned Thing!' he replied, without turning his head. His voice was husky and unnatural. He trembled visibly.

'I was about to speak further, when I observed the wild oats near the place of the disturbance moving in the most inexplicable way. I can hardly describe it. It seemed as if stirred by a streak of wind, which not only bent it, but pressed it down—crushed it so that it did not rise, and this movement was slowly prolonging itself directly toward us.

'Nothing that I had ever seen had affected me so strangely as this unfamiliar and unaccountable phenomenon, yet I am unable to recall any sense of fear. I remember—and tell it here because, singularly enough, I recollected it then—

that once, in looking carelessly out of an open window, I momentarily mistook a small tree close at hand for one of a group of larger trees at a little distance away. It looked the same size as the others, but, being more distinctly and sharply defined in mass and detail, seemed out of harmony with them. It was a mere falsification of the law of aerial perspective, but it startled, almost terrified me. We so rely upon the orderly operation of familiar natural laws that any seeming suspension of them is noted as a menace to our safety, a warning of unthinkable calamity. So now the apparently causeless movement of the herbage, and the slow, undeviating approach of the line of disturbance were distinctly disquieting. My companion appeared actually frightened, and I could hardly credit my senses when I saw him suddenly throw his gun to his shoulders and fire both barrels at the agitated grass! Before the smoke of the discharge had cleared away I heard a loud savage cry—a scream like that of a wild animal—and, flinging his gun upon the ground, Morgan sprang away and ran swiftly from the spot. At the same instant I was thrown violently to the ground by the impact of something unseen in the smoke—some soft, heavy substance that seemed thrown against me with great force.

'Before I could get upon my feet and recover my gun, which seemed to have been struck from my hands, I heard Morgan crying out as if in mortal agony, and mingling with his cries were such hoarse savage sounds as one hears from fighting dogs. Inexpressibly terrified, I struggled to my feet and looked in the direction of Morgan's retreat; and may heaven in mercy spare me from another sight like that! At a distance of less than thirty yards was my friend, down upon one knee, his head thrown back at a frightful angle, hatless, his long hair in disorder and his whole body in violent movement from side to side, backward and forward. His right arm was lifted and seemed to lack the hand—at least, I could see none. The other arm was invisible. At times, as my memory now reports this extraordinary scene, I could discern but a part of his body; it was as if he had been partly blotted out—I can not otherwise express it—then a shifting of his position would bring it all into view again.

'All this must have occurred within a few seconds, yet in that time Morgan assumed all the postures of a determined wrestler vanquished by superior weight and strength. I saw nothing but him, and him not always distinctly. During the entire incident his shouts and curses were heard, as if through an enveloping uproar of such sounds of rage and fury as I had never heard from the throat of man or brute!

'For a moment only I stood irresolute, then, throwing down my gun, I ran forward to my friend's assistance. I had a vague belief that he was suffering from a fit or some form of convulsion. Before I could reach his side he was down and quiet. All sounds had ceased, but, with a feeling of such terror as even these awful events had not inspired, I now saw the same mysterious movement of the wild oats prolonging itself from the trampled area about the prostrate man toward the edge of a wood. It was only when it had reached the wood that I was able to withdraw my eyes and look at my companion. He was dead.'

III

The coroner rose from his seat and stood beside the dead man. Lifting an edge of the sheet he pulled it away, exposing the entire body, altogether naked and showing in the candle light a clay–like yellow. It had, however, broad maculations of bluish–black, obviously caused by extravasated blood from contusions. The chest and sides looked as if they had been beaten with a bludgeon. There were dreadful lacerations; the skin was torn in strips and shreds.

The coroner moved round to the end of the table and undid a silk handkerchief, which had been passed under the chin and knotted on the top of the head. When the handkerchief was drawn away it exposed what had been the throat. Some of the jurors who had risen to get a better view repented their curiosity, and turned away their faces. Witness Harker went to the open window and leaned out across the sill, faint and sick. Dropping the handkerchief upon the dead man's neck, the coroner stepped to an angle of the room, and from a pile of clothing produced one garment after another, each of which he held up a moment for inspection. All were torn, and stiff with blood. The jurors did not make a closer inspection. They seemed rather uninterested. They had, in truth, seen all this before; the only thing that was new to them being Harker's testimony.

'Gentlemen,' the coroner said, 'we have no more evidence, I think. Your duty has been already explained to you; if there is nothing you wish to ask you may go outside and consider your verdict.'

The foreman rose—a tall, bearded man of sixty, coarsely clad.

'I should like to ask one question, Mr Coroner,' he said. 'What asylum did this yer last witness escape from?'

'Mr Harker,' said the coroner, gravely and tranquilly, 'from what asylum did you last escape?'

Harker flushed crimson again, but said nothing, and the seven jurors rose and solemnly filed out of the cabin.

'If you have done insulting me, sir,' said Harker, as soon as he and the officer were left alone with the dead man, 'I suppose I am at liberty to go?'

'Yes.'

Harker started to leave, but paused, with his hand on the door latch. The habit of his profession was strong in him—stronger than his sense of personal dignity. He turned about and said:

'The book that you have there—I recognize it as

Morgan's diary. You seemed greatly interested in it; you read in it while I was testifying. May I see it? The public would like—'

'The book will cut no figure in this matter,' replied the official, slipping it into his coat pocket; 'all the entries in it were made before the writer's death.'

As Harker passed out of the house the jury reentered and stood about the table on which the now covered corpse showed under the sheet with sharp definition. The foreman seated himself near the candle, produced from his breast pocket a pencil and scrap of paper, and wrote rather laboriously the following verdict, which with various degrees of effort all signed:

'We, the jury, do find that the remains come to their death at the hands of a mountain lion, but some of us thinks, all the same, they had fits.'

IV

In the diary of the late Hugh Morgan are certain interesting entries having, possibly, a scientific value as suggestions. At the inquest upon his body the book was not put in evidence; possibly the coroner thought it not worth while to confuse the jury. The date of the first of the entries mentioned can not be ascertained; the upper part of the leaf is torn away; the part of the entry remaining is as follows:

'... would run in a half circle, keeping his head turned

always toward the centre and again he would stand still, barking furiously. At last he ran away into the brush as fast as he could go. I thought at first that he had gone mad, but on returning to the house found no other alteration in his manner than what was obviously due to fear of punishment.

'Can a dog see with his nose? Do odors impress some olfactory centre with images of the thing emitting them?

'Sept 2.—Looking at the stars last night as they rose above the crest of the ridge east of the house, I observed them successively disappear—from left to right. Each was eclipsed but an instant, and only a few at the same time, but along the entire length of the ridge all that were within a degree or two of the crest were blotted out. It was as if something had passed along between me and them; but I could not see it, and the stars were not thick enough to define its outline. Ugh! I don't like this...'

Several weeks' entries are missing, three leaves being torn from the book.

'Sept. 27.—It has been about here again—I find evidences of its presence every day. I watched again all of last night in the same cover, gun in hand, double–charged with buckshot. In the morning the fresh footprints were there, as before. Yet I would have sworn that I did not sleep—indeed, I hardly sleep at all. It is terrible, insupportable! If these amazing experiences are real I shall go mad; if they are fanciful I am mad already.

'Oct. 3.—I shall not go—it shall not drive me away. No, this is my house, my land. God hates a coward....

'Oct. 5.—I can stand it no longer; I have invited Harker to pass a few weeks with me—he has a level head. I can judge from his manner if he thinks me mad.

'Oct. 7.—I have the solution of the problem; it came to me last night—suddenly, as by revelation. How simple—how terribly simple!

'There are sounds that we can not hear. At either end of the scale are notes that stir no chord of that imperfect instrument, the human ear. They are too high or too grave. I have observed a flock of blackbirds occupying an entire treetop—the tops of several trees—and all in full song. Suddenly—in a moment—at absolutely the same instant—all spring into the air and fly away. How? They could not all see one another—whole treetops intervened. At no point could a leader have been visible to all. There must have been a signal of warning or command, high and shrill above the din, but by me unheard. I have observed, too, the same simultaneous flight when all were silent, among not only blackbirds, but other birds—quail, for example, widely separated by bushes—even on opposite sides of a hill.

'It is known to seamen that a school of whales basking or sporting on the surface of the ocean, miles apart, with the convexity of the earth between them, will sometimes dive at the same instant—all gone out of sight in a moment.

The signal has been sounded—too grave for the ear of the sailor at the masthead and his comrades on the deck—who nevertheless feel its vibrations in the ship as the stones of a cathedral are stirred by the bass of the organ.

'As with sounds, so with colors. At each end of the solar spectrum the chemist can detect the presence of what are known as 'actinic' rays. They represent colors—integral colors in the composition of light—which we are unable to discern. The human eye is an imperfect instrument; its range is but a few octaves of the real 'chromatic scale' I am not mad; there are colors that we can not see.

'And, God help me! the Damned Thing is of such a color!'

Nathaniel Hawthorne
(1804-1864)

Wrote some of American literature's most famous works, including *The Scarlet Letter* and *The House of the Seven Gables.* His stories often explored Puritan New England and themes of guilt and sin. He worked as a customs official and was friends with many famous writers of his time.

The Birthmark
Nathaniel Hawthorne

In the latter part of the last century there lived a man of science, an eminent proficient in every branch of natural philosophy, who not long before our story opens had made experience of a spiritual affinity more attractive than any chemical one. He had left his laboratory to the care of an assistant, cleared his fine countenance from the furnace smoke, washed the stain of acids from his fingers, and persuaded a beautiful woman to become his wife. In those days when the comparatively recent discovery of electricity and other kindred mysteries of Nature seemed to open paths into the region of miracle, it was not unusual for the love of science to rival the love of woman in its depth and absorbing energy. The higher intellect, the imagination, the spirit, and even the heart might all find their congenial aliment in pursuits which, as some of their ardent votaries believed, would ascend from one step of powerful intelligence to another, until the philosopher should lay his hand on the secret of creative force and perhaps make new worlds for himself. We know not whether Aylmer possessed this degree of faith in man's ultimate control over Nature. He had devoted himself, however, too unreservedly to scientific studies ever to be weaned from them by any second passion. His love for his young wife might prove the stronger of the two; but it could only be by intertwining itself with his love of science, and uniting the strength of the latter to his own.

Such a union accordingly took place, and was attended with truly remarkable consequences and a deeply impressive moral. One day, very soon after their marriage, Aylmer sat gazing at his wife with a trouble in his countenance that grew stronger until he spoke.

'Georgiana,' said he, 'has it never occurred to you that the mark upon your cheek might be removed?'

'No, indeed,' said she, smiling; but perceiving the seriousness of his manner, she blushed deeply. 'To tell you the truth it has been so often called a charm that I was simple enough to imagine it might be so.'

'Ah, upon another face perhaps it might,' replied her husband; 'but never on yours. No, dearest Georgiana, you came so nearly perfect from the hand of Nature that this slightest possible defect, which we hesitate whether to term a defect or a beauty, shocks me, as being the visible mark of earthly imperfection.'

'Shocks you, my husband!' cried Georgiana, deeply

hurt; at first reddening with momentary anger, but then bursting into tears. 'Then why did you take me from my mother's side? You cannot love what shocks you!'

To explain this conversation it must be mentioned that in the centre of Georgiana's left cheek there was a singular mark, deeply interwoven, as it were, with the texture and substance of her face. In the usual state of her complexion—a healthy though delicate bloom—the mark wore a tint of deeper crimson, which imperfectly defined its shape amid the surrounding rosiness. When she blushed it gradually became more indistinct, and finally vanished amid the triumphant rush of blood that bathed the whole cheek with its brilliant glow. But if any shifting motion caused her to turn pale there was the mark again, a crimson stain upon the snow, in what Aylmer sometimes deemed an almost fearful distinctness. Its shape bore not a little similarity to the human hand, though of the smallest pygmy size. Georgiana's lovers were wont to say that some fairy at her birth hour had laid her tiny hand upon the infant's cheek, and left this impress there in token of the magic endowments that were to give her such sway over all hearts. Many a desperate swain would have risked life for the privilege of pressing his lips to the mysterious hand. It must not be concealed, however, that the impression wrought by this fairy sign manual varied exceedingly, according to the difference of temperament in the beholders. Some fastidious persons—but they were exclusively of her own sex—affirmed that the bloody hand, as they chose to call it, quite destroyed the effect of Georgiana's beauty, and rendered her countenance even hideous. But it would be as reasonable to say that one of those small blue stains which sometimes occur in the purest statuary marble would convert the Eve of Powers to a monster. Masculine observers, if the birthmark did not heighten their admiration, contented themselves with wishing it away, that the world might possess one living specimen of ideal loveliness without the semblance of a flaw. After his marriage,—for he thought little or nothing of the matter before,—Aylmer discovered that this was the case with himself.

Had she been less beautiful,—if Envy's self could have found aught else to sneer at,—he might have felt his affection heightened by the prettiness of this mimic hand, now vaguely portrayed, now lost, now stealing forth again and glimmering to and fro with every pulse of emotion that throbbed within her heart; but seeing her otherwise so perfect, he found this one defect grow more and more intolerable with every moment of their united lives. It was the fatal flaw of humanity which Nature, in one shape or another, stamps ineffaceably on all her productions, either to imply that they are temporary and finite, or that their perfection must be wrought by toil and pain. The crimson hand expressed the ineludible gripe in which mortality clutches the highest and purest of earthly mould, degrading them into kindred with the lowest, and even with the very brutes, like whom their visible frames return to dust. In this manner, selecting it as the symbol of his wife's liability to sin, sorrow, decay, and death, Aylmer's sombre imagination was not long in rendering the birthmark a frightful object, causing him more trouble and horror than ever Georgiana's beauty, whether of soul or sense, had given him delight.

At all the seasons which should have been their happiest, he invariably and without intending it, nay, in spite of a purpose to the contrary, reverted to this one disastrous topic. Trifling as it at first appeared, it so connected itself with innumerable trains of thought and modes of feeling that it became the central point of all. With the morning twilight Aylmer opened his eyes upon his wife's face and recognized the symbol of imperfection; and when they sat together at the evening hearth his eyes wandered stealthily to her cheek, and beheld, flickering with the blaze of the wood fire, the spectral hand that wrote mortality where he would fain have worshipped. Georgiana soon learned to shudder at his gaze. It needed but a glance with the peculiar expression that his face often wore to change the roses of her cheek into a deathlike paleness, amid which the crimson hand was brought strongly out, like a bass–relief of ruby on the whitest marble.

Late one night when the lights were growing dim, so as hardly to betray the stain on the poor wife's cheek, she herself, for the first time, voluntarily took up the subject.

'Do you remember, my dear Aylmer,' said she, with a feeble attempt at a smile, 'have you any recollection of a dream last night about this odious hand?'

'None! none whatever!' replied Aylmer, starting; but then he added, in a dry, cold tone, affected for the sake of concealing the real depth of his emotion, 'I might well dream of it; for before I fell asleep it had taken a pretty firm hold of my fancy.'

'And you did dream of it?' continued Georgiana, hastily; for she dreaded lest a gush of tears should interrupt what she had to say. 'A terrible dream! I wonder that you can forget it. Is it possible to forget this one expression?—'It is in her heart now; we must have it out!' Reflect, my husband; for by all means I would have you recall that dream.'

The mind is in a sad state when Sleep, the all-involving, cannot confine her spectres within the dim region of her sway, but suffers them to break forth, affrighting this actual life with secrets that perchance belong to a deeper one. Aylmer now remembered his dream. He had fancied himself with his servant Aminadab, attempting an operation for the removal of the birthmark; but the deeper went the knife, the deeper sank the hand, until at length its tiny grasp appeared to have caught hold of Georgiana's heart; whence, however, her husband was inexorably resolved to cut or wrench it away.

When the dream had shaped itself perfectly in his memory, Aylmer sat in his wife's presence with a guilty feeling. Truth often finds its way to the mind close muffled in robes of sleep, and then speaks with uncompromising directness of matters in regard to which we practise an unconscious self-deception during our waking moments. Until now he had not been aware of the tyrannizing influence acquired by one idea over his mind, and of the lengths which he might find in his heart to go for the sake of giving himself peace.

'Aylmer,' resumed Georgiana, solemnly, 'I know not what may be the cost to both of us to rid me of this fatal birthmark. Perhaps its removal may cause cureless deformity; or it may be the stain goes as deep as life itself. Again: do we know that there is a possibility, on any terms, of unclasping the firm gripe of this little hand which was laid upon me before I came into the world?'

'Dearest Georgiana, I have spent much thought upon the subject,' hastily interrupted Aylmer. 'I am convinced of the perfect practicability of its removal.'

'If there be the remotest possibility of it,' continued Georgiana, 'let the attempt be made at whatever risk. Danger is nothing to me; for life, while this hateful mark makes me the object of your horror and disgust,—life is a burden which I would fling down with joy. Either remove this dreadful hand, or take my wretched life! You have deep science. All the world bears witness of it.

'You have achieved great wonders. Cannot you remove this little, little mark, which I cover with the tips of two small fingers? Is this beyond your power, for the sake of your own peace, and to save your poor wife from madness?'

'Noblest, dearest, tenderest wife,' cried Aylmer, rapturously, 'doubt not my power. I have already given this matter the deepest thought—thought which might almost have enlightened me to create a being less perfect than yourself. Georgiana, you have led me deeper than ever into the heart of science. I feel myself fully competent to render this dear cheek as faultless as its fellow; and then, most beloved, what will be my triumph when I shall have corrected what Nature left imperfect in her fairest work! Even Pygmalion, when his sculptured woman assumed life, felt not greater ecstasy than mine will be.'

'It is resolved, then,' said Georgiana, faintly smiling. 'And, Aylmer, spare me not, though you should find the birthmark take refuge in my heart at last.'

Her husband tenderly kissed her cheek—her right cheek—not that which bore the impress of the crimson hand.

The next day Aylmer apprised his wife of a plan that he had formed whereby he might have opportunity for the intense thought and constant watchfulness which the proposed operation would require; while Georgiana, likewise, would enjoy the perfect repose essential to its success. They were to seclude themselves in the extensive apartments occupied by Aylmer as a laboratory, and where, during his toilsome youth, he had made discoveries in the elemental powers of Nature that had roused the admiration of all the learned societies in Europe. Seated calmly in this laboratory, the pale philosopher had investigated the secrets of the highest cloud region and of the profoundest mines; he had satisfied himself of the causes that kindled and kept alive the fires of the volcano; and had explained the mystery of fountains, and how it is that they gush forth, some so bright and pure, and others with such rich medicinal virtues, from the dark bosom of the earth. Here, too, at an earlier period, he had studied the wonders of the human frame, and attempted to fathom the very process by which Nature assimilates all her precious influences from earth and air, and from the spiritual world, to create and foster man, her masterpiece. The latter pursuit, however, Aylmer had long laid aside in unwilling recognition of the truth—against which all seekers sooner or later stumble—that our great creative Mother, while she amuses us with apparently working in the broadest sunshine, is yet severely careful to keep her own secrets, and, in spite of her pretended openness, shows us nothing but results. She permits us, indeed, to mar, but seldom to mend, and, like a jealous patentee, on no account to make. Now, however, Aylmer resumed these half-forgotten investigations; not, of course, with such hopes or wishes as first suggested them; but because they involved much physiological truth and lay in the path of his proposed scheme for the treatment of Georgiana.

As he led her over the threshold of the laboratory, Georgiana was cold and tremulous. Aylmer looked cheerfully into her face, with intent to reassure her, but was so startled with the intense glow of the birthmark upon the whiteness of her cheek that he could not restrain a strong convulsive shudder. His wife fainted.

'Aminadab! Aminadab!' shouted Aylmer, stamping violently on the floor.

Forthwith there issued from an inner apartment a man of low stature, but bulky frame, with shaggy hair hanging about his visage, which was grimed with the vapors of the furnace. This personage had been Aylmer's underworker during his whole scientific career, and was admirably fitted for that office by his great mechanical readiness, and the skill with which, while incapable of comprehending a single principle, he executed all the details of his master's experiments. With his vast strength, his shaggy hair, his smoky aspect, and the indescribable earthiness that incrusted him, he seemed to represent man's physical nature; while Aylmer's slender figure, and pale, intellectual face, were no less apt a type of the spiritual element.

'Throw open the door of the boudoir, Aminadab,' said Aylmer, 'and burn a pastil.'

'Yes, master,' answered Aminadab, looking intently at the lifeless form of Georgiana; and then he muttered to himself, 'If she were my wife, I'd never part with that birthmark.'

When Georgiana recovered consciousness she found herself breathing an atmosphere of penetrating fragrance, the gentle potency of which had recalled her from her deathlike faintness. The scene around her looked like enchantment. Aylmer had converted those smoky, dingy, sombre rooms, where he had spent his brightest years in recondite pursuits, into a series of beautiful apartments not unfit to be the secluded abode of a lovely woman. The walls were hung with gorgeous curtains, which imparted the combination of grandeur and grace that no other species of adornment can achieve; and as they fell from the ceiling to the floor, their rich and ponderous folds, concealing all angles and straight lines, appeared to shut in the scene from infinite space. For aught Georgiana knew, it might be a pavilion among the clouds. And Aylmer, excluding the sunshine, which would have interfered with his chemical processes, had supplied its place with perfumed lamps, emitting flames of various hue, but all uniting in a soft, impurpled radiance. He now knelt by his wife's side, watching her earnestly, but without alarm; for he was confident in his science, and felt that he could draw a magic circle round her within which no evil might intrude.

'Where am I? Ah, I remember,' said Georgiana, faintly; and she placed her hand over her cheek to hide the terrible mark from her husband's eyes.

'Fear not, dearest!' exclaimed he. 'Do not shrink from me! Believe me, Georgiana, I even rejoice in this single imperfection, since it will be such a rapture to remove it.'

'Oh, spare me!' sadly replied his wife. 'Pray do not look at it again. I never can forget that convulsive shudder.'

In order to soothe Georgiana, and, as it were, to release her mind from the burden of actual things, Aylmer now put in practice some of the light and playful secrets which science had taught him among its profounder lore. Airy figures, absolutely bodiless ideas, and forms of unsubstantial beauty came and danced before her, imprinting their momentary footsteps on beams of light. Though she had some indistinct idea of the method of these optical phenomena, still the illusion was almost perfect enough to warrant the belief that her husband possessed sway over the spiritual world. Then again, when she felt a wish to look forth from her seclusion, immediately, as if her thoughts were answered, the procession of external existence flitted across a screen. The scenery and the figures of actual life were perfectly represented, but with that bewitching, yet indescribable difference which always makes a picture, an image, or a shadow so much more attractive than the original. When wearied of this, Aylmer bade her cast her eyes upon a vessel containing a quantity of earth. She did so, with little interest at first; but was soon startled to perceive the germ of a plant shooting upward from the soil. Then came the slender stalk; the leaves gradually unfolded themselves; and amid them was a perfect and lovely flower.

'It is magical!' cried Georgiana. 'I dare not touch it.'

'Nay, pluck it,' answered Aylmer,—'pluck it, and inhale its brief perfume while you may. The flower will wither in a few moments and leave nothing save its brown seed vessels; but thence may be perpetuated a race as ephemeral as itself.'

But Georgiana had no sooner touched the flower than the whole plant suffered a blight, its leaves turning coal-black as if by the agency of fire.

'There was too powerful a stimulus,' said Aylmer, thoughtfully.

To make up for this abortive experiment, he proposed to take her portrait by a scientific process of his own invention. It was to be effected by rays of light striking upon a polished plate of metal. Georgiana assented; but, on looking at the result, was affrighted to find the features of the portrait blurred and indefinable; while the minute figure of a hand appeared where the cheek should have been. Aylmer snatched the metallic plate and threw it into a jar of corrosive acid.

Soon, however, he forgot these mortifying failures. In the intervals of study and chemical experiment he came to her flushed and exhausted, but seemed invigorated by her presence, and spoke in glowing language of the resources of his art. He gave a history of the long dynasty of the alchemists, who spent so many ages in quest of the universal solvent by which the golden principle might be elicited from all things vile and base. Aylmer appeared to believe that, by the plainest scientific logic, it was altogether within the limits of possibility to discover this long-sought medium; 'but,' he added, 'a philosopher who should go deep enough to acquire the power would attain too lofty a wisdom to stoop to the exercise of it.' Not less singular were his opinions in regard to the elixir vitae. He more than intimated that it was at his option to concoct a liquid that should prolong life for years, perhaps interminably; but that it would produce a discord in Nature which all the world, and chiefly the quaffer of the immortal nostrum, would find cause to curse.

'Aylmer, are you in earnest?' asked Georgiana, looking at him with amazement and fear. 'It is terrible to possess such power, or even to dream of possessing it.'

'Oh, do not tremble, my love,' said her husband. 'I would not wrong either you or myself by working such inharmonious effects upon our lives; but I would have you consider how trifling, in comparison, is the skill requisite to remove this little hand.'

At the mention of the birthmark, Georgiana, as usual, shrank as if a redhot iron had touched her cheek.

Again Aylmer applied himself to his labors. She could hear his voice in the distant furnace room giving directions to Aminadab, whose harsh, uncouth, misshapen tones were audible in response, more like the grunt or growl of a brute than human speech. After hours of absence, Aylmer reappeared and proposed that she should now examine his cabinet of chemical products and natural treasures of the earth. Among the former he showed her a small vial, in which, he remarked, was contained a gentle yet most powerful fragrance, capable of impregnating all the breezes that blow across a kingdom. They were of inestimable value, the contents of that little vial; and, as he said so, he threw some of the perfume into the air and filled the room with piercing and invigorating delight.

'And what is this?' asked Georgiana, pointing to a small crystal globe containing a gold–colored liquid. 'It is so beautiful to the eye that I could imagine it the elixir of life.'

'In one sense it is,' replied Aylmer; 'or, rather, the elixir of immortality. It is the most precious poison that ever was concocted in this world. By its aid I could apportion the lifetime of any mortal at whom you might point your finger. The strength of the dose would determine whether he were to linger out years, or drop dead in the midst of a breath. No king on his guarded throne could keep his life if I, in my private station, should deem that the welfare of millions justified me in depriving him of it.'

'Why do you keep such a terrific drug?' inquired Georgiana in horror.

'Do not mistrust me, dearest,' said her husband,

smiling; 'its virtuous potency is yet greater than its harmful one. But see! here is a powerful cosmetic. With a few drops of this in a vase of water, freckles may be washed away as easily as the hands are cleansed. A stronger infusion would take the blood out of the cheek, and leave the rosiest beauty a pale ghost.'

'Is it with this lotion that you intend to bathe my cheek?' asked Georgiana, anxiously.

'Oh, no,' hastily replied her husband; 'this is merely superficial. Your case demands a remedy that shall go deeper.'

In his interviews with Georgiana, Aylmer generally made minute inquiries as to her sensations and whether the confinement of the rooms and the temperature of the atmosphere agreed with her. These questions had such a particular drift that Georgiana began to conjecture that she was already subjected to certain physical influences, either breathed in with the fragrant air or taken with her food. She fancied likewise, but it might be altogether fancy, that there was a stirring up of her system—a strange, indefinite sensation creeping through her veins, and tingling, half painfully, half pleasurably, at her heart. Still, whenever she dared to look into the mirror, there she beheld herself pale as a white rose and with the crimson birthmark stamped upon her cheek. Not even Aylmer now hated it so much as she.

To dispel the tedium of the hours which her husband

found it necessary to devote to the processes of combination and analysis, Georgiana turned over the volumes of his scientific library. In many dark old tomes she met with chapters full of romance and poetry. They were the works of philosophers of the middle ages, such as Albertus Magnus, Cornelius Agrippa, Paracelsus, and the famous friar who created the prophetic Brazen Head. All these antique naturalists stood in advance of their centuries, yet were imbued with some of their credulity, and therefore were believed, and perhaps imagined themselves to have acquired from the investigation of Nature a power above Nature, and from physics a sway over the spiritual world. Hardly less curious and imaginative were the early volumes of the Transactions of the Royal Society, in which the members, knowing little of the limits of natural possibility, were continually recording wonders or proposing methods whereby wonders might be wrought.

But to Georgiana the most engrossing volume was a large folio from her husband's own hand, in which he had recorded every experiment of his scientific career, its original aim, the methods adopted for its development, and its final success or failure, with the circumstances to which either event was attributable. The book, in truth, was both the history and emblem of his ardent, ambitious, imaginative, yet practical and laborious life. He handled physical details as if there were nothing beyond them; yet spiritualized them all, and redeemed himself from materialism by his strong and eager aspiration towards the infinite. In his grasp the veriest clod of earth assumed a soul. Georgiana, as she read, reverenced Aylmer and loved him more profoundly than ever, but with a less entire dependence on his judgment than heretofore. Much as he had accomplished, she could not but observe that his most splendid successes were almost invariably failures, if compared with the ideal at which he aimed. His brightest diamonds were the merest pebbles, and felt to be so by himself, in comparison with the inestimable gems which lay hidden beyond his reach. The volume, rich with achievements that had won renown for its author, was yet as melancholy a record as ever mortal hand had penned. It was the sad confession and continual exemplification of the shortcomings of the composite man, the spirit burdened with clay and working in matter, and of the despair that assails the higher nature at finding itself so miserably thwarted by the earthly part. Perhaps every man of genius in whatever sphere might recognize the image of his own experience in Aylmer's journal.

So deeply did these reflections affect Georgiana that she laid her face upon the open volume and burst into tears. In this situation she was found by her husband.

'It is dangerous to read in a sorcerer's books,' said he with a smile, though his countenance was uneasy and displeased. 'Georgiana, there are pages in that volume which I can scarcely glance over and keep my senses. Take heed lest it prove as detrimental to you.'

'It has made me worship you more than ever,' said she.

'Ah, wait for this one success,' rejoined he, 'then worship me if you will. I shall deem myself hardly unworthy of it. But come, I have sought you for the luxury of your voice. Sing to me, dearest.'

So she poured out the liquid music of her voice to quench the thirst of his spirit. He then took his leave with a boyish exuberance of gayety, assuring her that her seclusion would endure but a little longer, and that the result was already certain. Scarcely had he departed when Georgiana felt irresistibly impelled to follow him. She had forgotten to inform Aylmer of a symptom which for two or three hours past had begun to excite her attention. It was a sensation in the fatal birthmark, not painful, but which induced a restlessness throughout her system. Hastening after her husband, she intruded for the first time into the laboratory.

The first thing that struck her eye was the furnace, that hot and feverish worker, with the intense glow of its fire, which by the quantities of soot clustered above it seemed to have been burning for ages. There was a distilling apparatus in full operation. Around the room were retorts, tubes, cylinders, crucibles, and other apparatus of chemical research. An electrical machine stood ready for immediate use. The atmosphere felt oppressively close, and was tainted with gaseous odors which had been tormented forth by the processes of science. The severe and homely simplicity of the apartment, with its naked walls and brick pavement, looked strange, accustomed as Georgiana had become to the fantastic elegance of her boudoir. But what chiefly, indeed almost solely, drew her attention, was the aspect of Aylmer himself.

He was pale as death, anxious and absorbed, and hung over the furnace as if it depended upon his utmost watchfulness whether the liquid which it was distilling should be the draught of immortal happiness or misery. How different from the sanguine and joyous mien that he had assumed for Georgiana's encouragement!

'Carefully now, Aminadab; carefully, thou human machine; carefully, thou man of clay!' muttered Aylmer, more to himself than his assistant. 'Now, if there be a thought too much or too little, it is all over.'

'Ho! ho!' mumbled Aminadab. 'Look, master! look!'

Aylmer raised his eyes hastily, and at first reddened, then grew paler than ever, on beholding Georgiana. He rushed towards her and seized her arm with a gripe that left the print of his fingers upon it.

'Why do you come hither? Have you no trust in your husband?' cried he, impetuously. 'Would you throw the blight of that fatal birthmark over my labors? It is not well done. Go, prying woman, go!'

'Nay, Aylmer,' said Georgiana with the firmness of which she possessed no stinted endowment, 'it is not you that have a right to complain. You mistrust your wife; you have concealed the anxiety with which you watch the development of this experiment. Think not so unworthily of me, my husband. Tell me all the risk we run, and fear not that I shall shrink; for my share in it is far less than your own.'

'No, no, Georgiana!' said Aylmer, impatiently; 'it must not be.'

'I submit,' replied she calmly. 'And, Aylmer, I shall quaff whatever draught you bring me; but it will be on the same principle that would induce me to take a dose of poison if offered by your hand.'

'My noble wife,' said Aylmer, deeply moved, 'I knew not the height and depth of your nature until now. Nothing shall be concealed. Know, then, that this crimson hand, superficial as it seems, has clutched its grasp into your being with a strength of which I had no previous conception. I have already administered agents powerful enough to do aught except to change your entire physical system. Only one thing remains to be tried. If that fail us we are ruined.'

'Why did you hesitate to tell me this?' asked she.

'Because, Georgiana,' said Aylmer, in a low voice, 'there is danger.'

'Danger? There is but one danger—that this horrible stigma shall be left upon my cheek!' cried Georgiana. 'Remove it, remove it, whatever be the cost, or we shall both go mad!'

'Heaven knows your words are too true,' said Aylmer, sadly. 'And now, dearest, return to your boudoir. In a little while all will be tested.'

He conducted her back and took leave of her with a solemn tenderness which spoke far more than his words how much was now at stake. After his departure Georgiana became rapt in musings. She considered the character of Aylmer, and did it completer justice than at any previous moment. Her heart exulted, while it trembled, at his honorable love—so pure and lofty that it would accept nothing less than perfection nor miserably make itself contented with an earthlier nature than he had dreamed of. She felt how much more precious was such a sentiment than that meaner kind which would have borne with the imperfection for her sake, and have been guilty of treason to holy love by degrading its perfect idea to the level of the actual; and with her whole spirit she prayed that, for a single moment, she might satisfy his highest and deepest conception. Longer than one moment she well knew it could not be; for his spirit was ever on the march, ever ascending, and each instant required something that was beyond the scope of the instant before.

The sound of her husband's footsteps aroused her. He bore a crystal goblet containing a liquor colorless as water, but bright enough to be the draught of immortality. Aylmer was pale; but it seemed rather the consequence of a highly-wrought state of mind and tension of spirit than of fear or doubt.

'The concoction of the draught has been perfect,' said he, in answer to Georgiana's look. 'Unless all my science have deceived me, it cannot fail.'

'Save on your account, my dearest Aylmer,' observed his wife, 'I might wish to put off this birthmark of mortality by relinquishing mortality itself in preference to any other mode. Life is but a sad possession to those who have attained precisely the degree of moral advancement at which I stand. Were I weaker and blinder it might be happiness. Were I stronger, it might be endured hopefully. But, being what I find myself, methinks I am of all mortals the most fit to die.'

'You are fit for heaven without tasting death!' replied her husband 'But why do we speak of dying? The draught cannot fail. Behold its effect upon this plant.'

On the window seat there stood a geranium diseased with yellow blotches, which had overspread all its leaves. Aylmer poured a small quantity of the liquid upon the soil in which it grew. In a little time, when the roots of the plant had taken up the moisture, the unsightly blotches began to be extinguished in a living verdure.

'There needed no proof,' said Georgiana, quietly. 'Give me the goblet I joyfully stake all upon your word.'

'Drink, then, thou lofty creature!' exclaimed Aylmer, with fervid admiration. 'There is no taint of imperfection on thy spirit. Thy sensible frame, too, shall soon be all perfect.'

She quaffed the liquid and returned the goblet to his hand.

'It is grateful,' said she with a placid smile. 'Methinks it is like water from a heavenly fountain; for it contains I know not what of unobtrusive fragrance and deliciousness. It allays a feverish thirst that had parched me for many days. Now, dearest, let me sleep. My earthly senses are closing over my spirit like the leaves around the heart of a rose at sunset.'

She spoke the last words with a gentle reluctance, as if it required almost more energy than she could command to pronounce the faint and lingering syllables. Scarcely had they loitered through her lips ere she was lost in slumber. Aylmer sat by her side, watching her aspect with the emotions proper to a man the whole value of whose existence was involved in the process now to be tested. Mingled with this mood, however, was the philosophic investigation characteristic of the man of science. Not the minutest symptom escaped him. A heightened flush of the cheek, a slight irregularity of breath, a quiver of the eyelid, a hardly perceptible tremor through the frame,—such were the details which, as the moments passed, he wrote down in his folio volume. Intense thought had set its stamp upon every previous page of that volume, but the thoughts of years were all concentrated upon the last.

While thus employed, he failed not to gaze often at the fatal hand, and not without a shudder. Yet once, by a strange and unaccountable impulse he pressed it with his lips. His spirit recoiled, however, in the very act, and Georgiana, out of the midst of her deep sleep, moved uneasily and murmured as if in remonstrance. Again Aylmer resumed his watch. Nor was it without avail. The crimson hand, which at first had been strongly visible upon the marble paleness of Georgiana's cheek, now grew more faintly outlined. She remained not less pale than ever; but the birthmark with every breath that came and went, lost somewhat of its former distinctness. Its presence had been awful; its departure was more awful still. Watch the stain of the rainbow fading out the sky, and you will know how that mysterious symbol passed away.

'By Heaven! it is well–nigh gone!' said Aylmer to himself, in almost irrepressible ecstasy. 'I can scarcely trace it now. Success! success! And now it is like the faintest rose color. The lightest flush of blood across her cheek would overcome it. But she is so pale!'

He drew aside the window curtain and suffered the light of natural day to fall into the room and rest upon her cheek. At the same time he heard a gross, hoarse chuckle, which he had long known as his servant Aminadab's expression of delight.

'Ah, clod! ah, earthly mass!' cried Aylmer, laughing in a sort of frenzy, 'you have served me well! Matter and spirit—earth and heaven—have both done their part in this! Laugh, thing of the senses! You have earned the right to laugh.'

These exclamations broke Georgiana's sleep. She slowly unclosed her eyes and gazed into the mirror which her husband had arranged for that purpose. A faint smile flitted over her lips when she recognized how barely perceptible was now that crimson hand which had once blazed forth with such disastrous brilliancy as to scare away all their happiness. But then her eyes sought Aylmer's face with a trouble and anxiety that he could by no means account for.

'My poor Aylmer!' murmured she.

'Poor? Nay, richest, happiest, most favored!' exclaimed he. 'My peerless bride, it is successful! You are perfect!'

'My poor Aylmer,' she repeated, with a more than human tenderness, 'you have aimed loftily; you have done nobly. Do not repent that with so high and pure a feeling, you have rejected the best the earth could offer. Aylmer, dearest Aylmer, I am dying!'

Alas! it was too true! The fatal hand had grappled with the mystery of life, and was the bond by which an angelic spirit kept itself in union with a mortal frame. As the last crimson tint of the birthmark—that sole token of human imperfection—faded from her cheek, the parting breath of the now perfect woman passed into the atmosphere, and her soul, lingering a moment near her husband, took its heavenward flight. Then a hoarse, chuckling laugh was heard again! Thus ever does the gross fatality of earth exult in its invariable triumph over the immortal essence which, in this dim sphere of half development, demands the completeness of a higher state. Yet, had Alymer reached a profounder wisdom, he need not thus have flung away the happiness which would have woven his mortal life of the selfsame texture with the celestial. The momentary circumstance was too strong for him; he failed to look beyond the shadowy scope of time, and, living once for all in eternity, to find the perfect future in the present.

Mary Shelley
(1797-1851)

Created the science fiction masterpiece *Frankenstein* when she was just 18, after a famous ghost story competition with Lord Byron and others. She was married to the poet Percy Shelley and faced numerous personal tragedies but continued writing throughout her life.

The Mortal Immortal

Mary Shelley

July 16, 1833—This is a memorable anniversary for me; on it I complete my three hundred and twenty–third year!

The Wandering Jew?—certainly not. More than eighteen centuries have passed over his head. In comparison with him, I am a very young Immortal.

Am I, then, immortal? This is a question which I have asked myself, by day and night, for now three hundred and three years, and yet cannot answer it. I detected a grey hair amidst my brown locks this very day—that surely signifies decay. Yet it may have remained concealed there for three hundred years—for some persons have become entirely white-headed before twenty years of age.

I will tell my story, and my reader shall judge for me. I will tell my story, and so contrive to pass some few hours of a long eternity, become so wearisome to me. For ever! Can it be? to live for ever! I have heard of enchantments, in which the victims were plunged into a deep sleep, to wake, after a hundred years, as fresh as ever: I have heard of the Seven Sleepers—thus to be immortal would not be so burthensome: but, oh! the weight of never–ending time—the tedious passage of the still–succeeding hours! How happy was the fabled Nourjahad!—But to my task.

All the world has heard of Cornelius Agrippa. His memory is as immortal as his arts have made me. All the world has also heard of his scholar, who, unawares, raised the foul fiend during his master's absence, and was destroyed by him. The report, true or false, of this accident, was attended with many inconveniences to the renowned philosopher. All his scholars at once deserted him—his servants disappeared. He had no one near him to put coals on his ever-burning fires while he slept, or to attend to the changeful colours of his medicines while he studied. Experiment after experiment failed, because one pair of hands was insufficient to complete them: the dark spirits laughed at him for not being able to retain a single mortal in his service.

I was then very young—very poor—and very much in love. I had been for about a year the pupil of Cornelius, though I was absent when this accident took place. On my return, my friends implored me not to return to the alchymist's abode. I trembled as I listened to the dire tale they told; I required no second warning; and when Cornelius came and offered me a purse of gold if I would remain under his roof, I felt as if Satan himself tempted me. My teeth chattered—my hair stood on end;—I ran off as fast as my trembling knees would permit.

My failing steps were directed whither for two years they had every evening been attracted,—a gently bubbling spring of pure living water, beside which lingered a dark–haired girl, whose beaming eyes were fixed on the path I was accustomed each night to tread. I cannot remember the hour when I did not love Bertha; we had been neighbours and playmates from infancy,—her parents, like mine were of humble life, yet respectable,—our attachment had been a source of pleasure to them. In an evil hour, a malignant fever carried off both her father and mother, and Bertha became an orphan. She would have found a home beneath my paternal roof, but, unfortunately, the old lady of the near castle, rich, childless, and solitary, declared her intention to adopt her. Henceforth Bertha was clad in silk—inhabited a marble palace—and was looked on as being highly favoured by fortune. But in her new situation among her new associates, Bertha remained true to the friend of her humbler days; she often visited the cottage of my father, and when forbidden to go thither, she would stray towards the neighbouring wood, and meet me beside its shady fountain.

She often declared that she owed no duty to her new protectress equal in sanctity to that which bound us. Yet still I was too poor to marry, and she grew weary of being tormented on my account. She had a haughty but an impatient spirit, and grew angry at the obstacle that prevented our union. We met now after an absence, and she had been sorely beset while I was away; she complained bitterly, and almost reproached me for being poor. I replied hastily,—

'I am honest, if I am poor!—were I not, I might soon become rich!'

This exclamation produced a thousand questions. I feared to shock her by owning the truth, but she drew it from me; and then, casting a look of disdain on me, she said,—

'You pretend to love, and you fear to face the Devil for my sake!'

I protested that I had only dreaded to offend her;—while she dwelt on the magnitude of the reward that I should receive. Thus encouraged—shamed by her—led on by love and hope, laughing at my later fears, with quick steps and a light heart, I returned to accept the offers of the alchymist, and was instantly installed in my office.

A year passed away. I became possessed of no insignificant sum of money. Custom had banished my fears. In spite of the most painful vigilance, I had never detected the trace of a cloven foot; nor was the studious silence of our abode ever disturbed by demoniac howls. I still continued my stolen interviews with Bertha, and Hope dawned on me—Hope—but not perfect joy: for Bertha fancied that love and security were enemies, and her pleasure was to divide them in my bosom. Though true of heart, she was something of a coquette in manner; I was jealous as a Turk. She slighted me in a thousand ways, yet would never acknowledge herself to be in the wrong. She would drive me mad with anger, and then force me to beg her pardon. Sometimes she fancied that I was not sufficiently submissive, and then she had some story of a rival, favoured by her protectress. She was surrounded by silk–clad youths—the rich and gay. What chance had the sad–robed scholar of Cornelius compared with these?

On one occasion, the philosopher made such large demands upon my time, that I was unable to meet her as I was wont. He was engaged in some mighty work, and I was forced to remain, day and night, feeding his furnaces and watching his chemical preparations. Bertha waited for me in vain at the fountain. Her haughty spirit fired at this neglect; and when at last I stole out during a few short minutes allotted to me for slumber, and hoped to be consoled by her, she received me with disdain, dismissed me in scorn, and vowed that any man should possess her hand rather than he who could not be in two places at once for her sake. She would be revenged! And truly she was. In my dingy retreat I heard that she had been hunting, attended by Albert Hoffer. Albert Hoffer was favoured by her protectress, and the three passed in cavalcade before my smoky window. Methought that they mentioned my name; it was followed by a laugh of derision, as her dark eyes glanced contemptuously towards my abode.

Jealousy, with all its venom and all its misery, entered my breast. Now I shed a torrent of tears, to think that I should never call her mine; and, anon, I imprecated a thousand curses on her inconstancy. Yet, still I must stir the fires of the alchymist, still attend on the changes of his unintelligible medicines.

Cornelius had watched for three days and nights, nor closed his eyes. The progress of his alembics was slower than he expected: in spite of his anxiety, sleep weighted upon his eyelids. Again and again he threw off drowsiness with more than human energy; again and again it stole away his senses. He eyed his crucibles wistfully. 'Not ready yet,' he murmured; 'will another night pass before the work is accomplished? Winzy, you are vigilant—you are faithful—you have slept, my boy—you slept last night. Look at that glass vessel. The liquid it contains is of a soft rose–colour: the moment it begins to change hue, awaken me—till then I may close my eyes. First, it will turn white, and then emit golden flashes; but wait not till then; when the rose–colour fades, rouse me.' I scarcely heard the last words, muttered, as they were, in sleep. Even then he did not quite yield to nature. 'Winzy, my boy,' he again said,

'do not touch the vessel—do not put it to your lips; it is a philtre—a philtre to cure love; you would not cease to love your Bertha—beware to drink!'

And he slept. His venerable head sunk on his breast,

and I scarce heard his regular breathing. For a few minutes I watched the vessel—the rosy hue of the liquid remained unchanged. Then my thoughts wandered—they visited the fountain, and dwelt on a thousand charming scenes never to be renewed—never! Serpents and adders were in my heart as the word 'Never!' half formed itself on my lips. False girl!—false and cruel! Never more would she smile on me as that evening she smiled on Albert. Worthless, detested woman! I would not remain unrevenged—she should see Albert expire at her feet—she should die beneath my vengeance. She had smiled in disdain and triumph—she knew my wretchedness and her power. Yet what power had she?—the power of exciting my hate—my utter scorn—my—oh, all but indifference! Could I attain that—could I regard her with careless eyes, transferring my rejected love to one fairer and more true, that were indeed a victory!

A bright flash darted before my eyes. I had forgotten the medicine of the adept; I gazed on it with wonder: flashes of admirable beauty, more bright than those which the diamond emits when the sun's rays are on it, glanced from the surface of the liquid; and odour the most fragrant and grateful stole over my sense; the vessel seemed one globe of living radiance, lovely to the eye, and most inviting to the taste. The first thought, instinctively inspired by the grosser sense, was, I will—I must drink. I raised the vessel to my lips. 'It will cure me of love—of torture!'

Already I had quaffed half of the most delicious liquor ever tasted by the palate of man, when the philosopher stirred. I started—I dropped the glass—the fluid flamed and glanced along the floor, while I felt Cornelius's gripe at my throat, as he shrieked aloud, 'Wretch! you have destroyed the labour of my life!'

The philosopher was totally unaware that I had drunk any portion of his drug. His idea was, and I gave a tacit assent to it, that I had raised the vessel from curiosity, and that, frightened at its brightness, and the flashes of intense light it gave forth, I had let it fall. I never undeceived him. The fire of the medicine was quenched—the fragrance died away—he grew calm, as a philosopher should under the heaviest trials, and dismissed me to rest.

I will not attempt to describe the sleep of glory and bliss which bathed my soul in paradise during the remaining hours of that memorable night. Words would be faint and shallow types of my enjoyment, or of the gladness that possessed my bosom when I woke. I trod air—my thoughts were in heaven. Earth appeared heaven, and my inheritance upon it was to be one trance of delight. 'This it is to be cured of love,' I thought; 'I will see Bertha this day, and she will find her lover cold and regardless; too happy to be disdainful, yet how utterly indifferent to her!'

The hours danced away. The philosopher, secure that he had once succeeded, and believing that he might again, began to concoct the same medicine once more. He was shut up with his books and drugs, and I had a holiday. I dressed myself with care; I looked in an old but polished shield which served me for a mirror; methoughts my good looks had wonderfully improved. I hurried beyond the precincts of the town, joy in my soul, the beauty of heaven and earth around me. I turned my steps toward the castle—I could look on its lofty turrets with lightness of heart, for I was cured of love. My Bertha saw me afar off, as I came up the avenue. I know not what sudden impulse animated her bosom, but at the sight, she sprung with a light fawn–like bound down the marble steps, and was hastening towards me. But I had been perceived by another person. The old high–born hag, who called herself her protectress, and was her tyrant, had seen me also; she hobbled, panting, up the terrace; a page, as ugly as herself, held up her train, and fanned her as she hurried along, and stopped my fair girl with a 'How, now, my bold mistress? whither so fast? Back to your cage—hawks are abroad!'

Bertha clasped her hands—her eyes were still bent on my approaching figure. I saw the contest. How I abhorred the old crone who checked the kind impulses of my Bertha's softening heart. Hitherto, respect for her rank had caused me to avoid the lady of the castle; now I disdained such trivial considerations. I was cured of love, and lifted above all human fears; I hastened forwards, and soon reached the terrace. How lovely Bertha looked! her eyes flashing fire, her cheeks glowing with impatience and anger, she was a thousand times more graceful and charming than ever. I no longer loved—oh no! I adored—worshipped—idolized her!

She had that morning been persecuted, with more than usual vehemence, to consent to an immediate marriage with my rival. She was reproached with the encouragement that she had shown him—she was threatened with being turned out of doors with disgrace and shame. Her proud spirit rose in arms at the threat; but when she remembered the scorn that she had heaped upon me, and how, perhaps, she had thus lost one whom she now regarded as her only friend, she wept with remorse and rage. At that moment I appeared. 'Oh, Winzy!' she exclaimed, 'take me to your mother's cot; swiftly let me leave the detested luxuries and wretchedness of this noble dwelling—take me to poverty and happiness.'

I clasped her in my arms with transport. The old dame was speechless with fury, and broke forth into invective only when we were far on the road to my natal cottage. My mother received the fair fugitive, escaped from a gilt cage to nature and liberty, with tenderness and joy; my father, who loved her, welcomed her heartily; it was a day of rejoicing, which did not need the addition of the celestial potion of the alchymist to steep me in delight.

Soon after this eventful day, I became the husband of Bertha. I ceased to be the scholar of Cornelius, but I continued his friend. I always felt grateful to him for having, unaware, procured me that delicious draught of a divine elixir, which, instead of curing me of love (sad cure! solitary and joyless remedy for evils which seem blessings to the memory), had inspired me with courage and resolution, thus winning for me an inestimable treasure in my Bertha.

I often called to mind that period of trance–like inebriation with wonder. The drink of Cornelius had not fulfilled the task for which he affirmed that it had been prepared, but its effects were more potent and blissful than words can express. They had faded by degrees, yet they lingered long—and painted life in hues of splendour. Bertha often wondered at my lightness of heart and unaccustomed gaiety; for, before, I had been rather serious, or even sad, in my disposition. She loved me the better for my cheerful temper, and our days were winged by joy.

Five years afterwards I was suddenly summoned to the bedside of the dying Cornelius. He had sent for me in haste, conjuring my instant presence. I found him stretched on his pallet, enfeebled even to death; all of life that yet remained animated his piercing eyes, and they were fixed on a glass vessel, full of roseate liquid.

'Behold,' he said, in a broken and inward voice, 'the vanity of human wishes! a second time my hopes are about to be crowned, a second time they are destroyed. Look at that liquor—you may remember five years ago I had prepared the same, with the same success;— then, as now, my thirsting lips expected to taste the immortal elixir —you dashed it from me! and at present it is too late.'

He spoke with difficulty, and fell back on his pillow. I could not help saying,—

'How, revered master, can a cure for love restore you to life?'

A faint smile gleamed across his face as I listened earnestly to his scarcely intelligible answer.

'A cure for love and for all things—the Elixir of Immortality. Ah! if now I might drink, I should live for ever!'

As he spoke, a golden flash gleamed from the fluid; a well–remembered fragrance stole over the air; he raised himself, all weak as he was—strength seemed miraculously to re–enter his frame— he stretched forth his hand—a loud explosion startled me—a ray of fire shot up from the elixir, and the glass vessel which contained it was shivered to atoms! I turned my eyes towards the philosopher; he had fallen back—his eyes were glassy—his features rigid—he was dead!

But I lived, and was to live for ever! So said the unfortunate alchymist, and for a few days I believed his words. I remembered the glorious intoxication that had followed my stolen draught. I reflected on the change I had felt in my frame—in my soul. The bounding elasticity of the one—the buoyant lightness of the other. I surveyed myself in a mirror, and could perceive no change in my features during the space of the five years which had elapsed. I remembered the radiant hues and grateful scent of that delicious beverage—worthy the gift it was capable of bestowing—I was, then, IMMORTAL!

A few days after I laughed at my credulity. The old proverb, that 'a prophet is least regarded in his own country,' was true with respect to me and my defunct master. I loved him as a man—I respected him as a sage—but I derided the notion that he could command the powers of darkness, and laughed at the superstitious fears with which he was regarded by the vulgar. He was a wise philosopher, but had no acquaintance with any spirits but those clad in flesh and blood. His science was simply human; and human science, I soon persuaded myself, could never conquer nature's laws so far as to imprison the soul for ever within its carnal habitation. Cornelius had brewed a soul-refreshing drink—more inebriating than wine—sweeter and more fragrant than any fruit: it possessed probably strong medicinal powers, imparting gladness to the heart and vigour to the limbs; but its effects would wear out; already they were diminished in my frame. I was a lucky fellow to have quaffed health and joyous spirits, and perhaps a long life, at my master's hands; but my good fortune ended there: longevity was far different from immortality.

I continued to entertain this belief for many years. Sometimes a thought stole across me—Was the alchymist indeed deceived? But my habitual credence was, that I should meet the fate of all the children of Adam at my appointed time—a little late, but still at a natural age. Yet it was certain that I retained a wonderfully youthful look. I was laughed at for my vanity in consulting the mirror so often, but I consulted it in vain—my brow was untrenched—my cheeks—my eyes—my whole person continued as untarnished as in my twentieth year.

I was troubled. I looked at the faded beauty of Bertha—I seemed more like her son. By degrees our neighbors began to make similar observations, and I found at last that I went by the name of the Scholar bewitched. Bertha herself grew uneasy. She became jealous and peevish, and at length she began to question me. We had no children; we were all in all to each other; and though, as she grew older, her vivacious spirit became a little allied to ill–temper, and her beauty sadly diminished, I cherished her in my heart as the mistress I idolized, the wife I had sought and won with such perfect love.

At last our situation became intolerable: Bertha was fifty—I twenty years of age. I had, in very shame, in some measure adopted the habits of advanced age; I no longer mingled in the dance among the young and gay, but my heart bounded along with them while I restrained my feet; and a sorry figure I cut among the Nestors of our village. But before the time I mention, things were altered—we were universally shunned; we were—at least, I was—reported to have kept up an iniquitous acquaintance with some of my former master's supposed friends. Poor Bertha was pitied, but deserted. I was regarded with horror and detestation.

What was to be done? we sat by our winter fire—poverty had made itself felt, for none would buy the produce of my farm; and often I had been forced to journey twenty miles to some place where I was not known, to dispose of our property. It is true, we had saved something for an evil day—that day was come.

We sat by our lone fireside—the old–hearted youth and his antiquated wife. Again Bertha insisted on knowing the truth; she recapitulated all she had ever heard said about me, and added her own observations. She conjured me to cast off the spell; she described how much more comely grey hairs were than my chestnut locks; she descanted on the reverence and respect due to age—how preferable to the slight regard paid to mere children: could I imagine that the despicable gifts of youth and good looks outweighed disgrace, hatred and scorn? Nay, in the end I should be burnt as a dealer in the black art, while she, to whom I had not deigned to communicate any portion of my good fortune, might be stoned as my accomplice. At length she insinuated that I must share my secret with her, and bestow on her like benefits to those I myself enjoyed, or she would denounce me—and then she burst into tears.

Thus beset, methought it was the best way to tell the truth. I reveled it as tenderly as I could, and spoke only of a very long life, not of immortality—which representation, indeed, coincided best with my own ideas. When I ended I rose and said,—

'And now, my Bertha, will you denounce the lover of your youth?—You will not, I know. But it is too hard, my poor wife, that you should suffer for my ill–luck and the accursed arts of Cornelius. I will leave you—you have wealth enough, and friends will return in my absence. I will go; young as I seem and strong as I am, I can work and gain my bread among strangers, unsuspected and unknown. I loved you in youth; God is my witness that I would not desert you in age, but that your safety and happiness require it.'

I took my cap and moved toward the door; in a moment Bertha's arms were round my neck, and her lips were pressed to mine. 'No, my husband, my Winzy,' she said, 'you shall not go alone—take me with you; we will remove from this place, and, as you say, among strangers we shall be unsuspected and safe. I am not so old as quite to shame you, my Winzy; and I daresay the charm will soon wear off, and, with the blessing of God, you will become more elderly–looking, as is fitting; you shall not leave me.'

I returned the good soul's embrace heartily. 'I will not, my Bertha; but for your sake I had not thought of such a thing. I will be your true, faithful husband while you are spared to me, and do my duty by you to the last.'

The next day we prepared secretly for our emigration. We were obliged to make great pecuniary sacrifices—it could not be helped. We realized a sum sufficient, at least, to maintain us while Bertha lived; and, without saying adieu to any one, quitted our native country to take refuge in a remote part of western France.

It was a cruel thing to transport poor Bertha from her native village, and the friends of her youth, to a new country, new language, new customs. The strange secret of my destiny rendered this removal immaterial to me; but I compassionated her deeply, and was glad to perceive that she found compensation for her misfortunes in a variety of little ridiculous circumstances. Away from all tell–tale chroniclers, she sought to decrease the apparent disparity of our ages by a thousand feminine arts—rouge, youthful dress, and assumed juvenility of manner. I could not be angry. Did I not myself wear a mask? Why quarrel with hers, because it was less successful? I grieved deeply when I remembered that this was my Bertha, whom I had loved so fondly and won with such transport—the dark–eyed, dark–haired girl, with smiles of enchanting archness and a step like a fawn—this mincing, simpering, jealous old woman. I should have revered her grey locks and withered cheeks; but thus!—It was my work, I knew; but I did not the less deplore this type of human weakness.

Her jealously never slept. Her chief occupation was to discover that, in spite of outward appearances, I was myself growing old. I verily believe that the poor soul loved me truly in her heart, but never had woman so tormenting a mode of displaying fondness. She would discern wrinkles in my face and decrepitude in my walk, while I bounded along in youthful vigour, the youngest looking of twenty youths. I never dared address another woman. On one occasion, fancying that the belle of the village regarded me with favouring eyes, she brought me a grey wig. Her constant discourse among her acquaintances was, that though I looked so young, there was ruin at work within my frame; and she affirmed that the worst symptom about me was my apparent health. My youth was a disease, she said, and I ought at all times to prepare, if not for a sudden and awful death, at least to awake some morning white–headed and bowed down with all the marks of advanced years. I let her talk—I often joined in her conjectures. Her warnings chimed in with my never–ceasing speculations concerning my state, and I took an earnest, though painful, interest in listening to all that her quick wit and excited imagination could say on the subject.

Why dwell on these minute circumstances? We lived on for many long years. Bertha became bedrid and paralytic; I nursed her as a mother might a child. She grew peevish, and still harped upon one string—of how long I should survive her. It has ever been a source of consolation to me, that I performed my duty scrupulously towards her. She had been mine in youth, she was mine in age; and at last, when I heaped the sod over her corpse, I wept to feel that I had lost all that really bound me to humanity.

Since then how many have been my cares and woes, how few and empty my enjoyments! I pause here in my history—I will pursue it no further. A sailor without rudder or compass, tossed on a stormy sea—a traveller lost on a widespread heath, without landmark or stone to guide him—such I have been: more lost, more hopeless than either. A nearing ship, a gleam from some far cot, may save them; but I have no beacon except the hope of death.

Death! mysterious, ill–visaged friend of weak humanity! Why alone of all mortals have you cast me from your sheltering fold? Oh, for the peace of the grave! the deep silence of the iron–bound tomb! that thought would cease to work in my brain, and my heart beat no more with emotions varied only by new forms of sadness!

Am I immortal? I return to my first question. In the first place, is it not more probably that the beverage of the alchymist was fraught rather with longevity than eternal life? Such is my hope. And then be it remembered, that I only drank half of the potion prepared by him. Was not the whole necessary to complete the charm? To have drained half the Elixir of Immortality is but to be half–immortal—my Forever is thus truncated and null.

But again, who shall number the years of the half of eternity? I often try to imagine by what rule the infinite may be divided. Sometimes I fancy age advancing upon me. One grey hair I have found. Fool! do I lament? Yes, the fear of age and death often creeps coldly into my heart; and the more I live, the more I dread death, even while I abhor life. Such an enigma is man—born to perish—when he wars, as I do, against the established laws of his nature.

But for this anomaly of feeling surely I might die: the medicine of the alchymist would not be proof against fire—sword—and the strangling waters. I have gazed upon the blue depths of many a placid lake, and the tumultuous rushing of many a mighty river, and have said, peace inhabits those waters; yet I have turned my steps away, to live yet another day. I have asked myself, whether suicide would be a crime in one to whom thus only the portals of the other world could be opened. I have done all, except presenting myself as a soldier or duelist, an objection of destruction to my—no, not my fellow mortals, and therefore I have shrunk away. They are not my fellows. The inextinguishable power of life in my frame, and their ephemeral existence, places us wide as the poles asunder. I could not raise a hand against the meanest or the most powerful among them.

Thus have I lived on for many a year—alone, and weary of myself—desirous of death, yet never dying—a mortal immortal. Neither ambition nor avarice can enter my mind, and the ardent love that gnaws at my heart, never to be returned—never to find an equal on which to expend itself—lives there only to torment me.

This very day I conceived a design by which I may end all—without self-slaughter, without making another man a Cain—an expedition, which mortal frame can never survive, even endued with the youth and strength that inhabits mine. Thus I shall put my immortality to the test, and rest for ever—or return, the wonder and benefactor of the human species.

Before I go, a miserable vanity has caused me to pen these pages. I would not die, and leave no name behind. Three centuries have passed since I quaffed the fatal beverage; another year shall not elapse before, encountering gigantic dangers—warring with the powers of frost in their home—beset by famine, toil, and tempest—I yield this body, too tenacious a cage for a soul which thirsts for freedom, to the destructive elements of air and water; or, if I survive, my name shall be recorded as one of the most famous among the sons of men; and, my task achieved, I shall adopt more resolute means, and, by scattering and annihilating the atoms that compose my frame, set at liberty the life imprisoned within, and so cruelly prevented from soaring from this dim earth to a sphere more congenial to its immortal essence.

Edgar Allan Poe

(1809-1849)

He revolutionised horror, mystery, and detective fiction. He lived a troubled life marked by poverty and tragedy but produced enduring works like *The Raven,* The *Tell-Tale Heart,* and *The Fall of the House of Usher.* He died under mysterious circumstances in Baltimore.

The Conversation of Eiros and Charmion

Edgar Allan Poe

Πυρ σοι προσοισω.
I will bring fire to thee.
—EURIPIDES—Androm

EIROS: Why do you call me Eiros?
CHARMION: So henceforward will you always be called. You must forget too, my earthly name, and speak to me as Charmion.
EIROS: This is indeed no dream!
CHARMION: Dreams are with us no more; but of these mysteries anon. I rejoice to see you looking life–like and rational. The film of the shadow has already passed from off your eyes. Be of heart and fear nothing. Your allotted days of stupor have expired and, tomorrow, I will myself induct you into the full joys and wonders of your novel existence.

EIROS: True—I feel no stupor—none at all. The wild sickness and the terrible darkness have left me, and I hear no longer that mad, rushing, horrible sound, like the 'voice of many waters.' Yet my senses are bewildered, Charmion, with the keenness of their perception of the new.

CHARMION: A few days will remove all this;—but I fully understand you, and feel for you. It is now ten earthly years since I underwent what you undergo—yet the remembrance of it hangs by me still. You have now suffered all of pain, however, which you will suffer in Aidenn.

EIROS: In Aidenn?

CHARMION: In Aidenn.

EIROS: Oh God!—pity me, Charmion!—I am overburthened with the majesty of all things—of the unknown now known—of the speculative Future merged in the august and certain Present.

CHARMION: Grapple not now with such thoughts. Tomorrow we will speak of this. Your mind wavers, and its agitation will find relief in the exercise of simple memories. Look not around, nor forward—but back. I am burning with anxiety to hear the details of that stupendous event which threw you among us. Tell me of it. Let us converse of familiar things, in the old familiar language of the world which has so fearfully perished.

EIROS: Most fearfully, fearfully!—this is indeed no dream.

CHARMION: Dreams are no more. Was I much mourned, my Eiros?

EIROS: Mourned, Charmion?—oh deeply. To that last hour of all, there hung a cloud of intense gloom and devout sorrow over your household.

CHARMION: And that last hour—speak of it. Remember that, beyond the naked fact of the catastrophe itself, I know nothing. When, coming out from among mankind, I passed into Night through the Grave—at that period, if I remember aright, the calamity which overwhelmed you was utterly unanticipated. But, indeed, I knew little of the speculative philosophy of the day.

EIROS: The individual calamity was as you say entirely unanticipated; but analogous misfortunes had been long a subject of discussion with astronomers. I need scarce tell you, my friend, that, even when you left us, men had agreed to understand those passages in the most holy writings which speak of the final destruction of all things by fire, as having reference to the orb of the earth alone. But in regard to the immediate agency of the ruin, speculation had been at fault from that epoch in astronomical knowledge in which the comets were divested of the terrors of flame. The very moderate density of these bodies had been well established. They had been observed to pass among the satellites of Jupiter, without bringing about any sensible alteration either in the masses or in the orbits of these secondary planets. We had long regarded the wanderers as vapory creations of inconceivable tenuity, and as altogether incapable of doing injury to our substantial globe, even in the event of contact. But contact was not in any degree dreaded; for the elements of all the comets were accurately known. That among them we should look for the agency of the threatened fiery destruction had been for many years considered an inadmissible idea. But wonders and wild fancies had been, of late days, strangely rife among mankind; and, although it was only with a few of the ignorant that actual apprehension prevailed, upon the announcement by astronomers of a new comet, yet this announcement was generally received with I know not what of agitation and mistrust.

The elements of the strange orb were immediately calculated, and it was at once conceded by all observers, that its path, at perihelion, would bring it into very close proximity with the earth. There were two or three astronomers, of secondary note, who resolutely maintained that a contact was inevitable. I cannot very well express to you the effect of this intelligence upon the people. For a few short days they would not believe an assertion which their intellect so long employed among worldly considerations could not in any manner grasp. But the truth of a vitally important fact soon makes its way into the understanding of even the most stolid. Finally, all men saw that astronomical knowledge lied not, and they awaited the comet. Its approach was not, at first, seemingly rapid; nor was its appearance of very unusual character. It was of a dull red, and had little perceptible train. For seven or eight days we saw no material increase in its apparent diameter, and but a partial alteration in its color. Meantime, the ordinary affairs of men were discarded and all interests absorbed in a growing discussion, instituted by the philosophic, in respect to the cometary nature. Even the grossly ignorant aroused their sluggish capacities to such considerations. The learned now gave their intellect—their soul—to no such points as the allaying of fear, or to the sustenance of loved theory. They sought—they panted for right views. They groaned for perfected knowledge. Truth arose in the purity of her strength and exceeding majesty, and the wise bowed down and adored.

That material injury to our globe or to its inhabitants would result from the apprehended contact, was an opinion which hourly lost ground among the wise; and the wise were now freely permitted to rule the reason and the fancy of the crowd. It was demonstrated, that the density of the comet's nucleus was far less than that of our rarest gas; and the harmless passage of a similar visitor among the satellites of Jupiter was a point strongly insisted upon, and which served greatly to allay terror. Theologists with an earnestness fear–enkindled, dwelt upon the biblical prophecies, and expounded them to the people with a directness and simplicity of which no previous instance had been known. That the final destruction of the earth must be brought about by the agency of fire, was urged with a spirit that enforced every where conviction; and that the comets were of no fiery nature (as all men now knew) was a truth which relieved all, in a great measure, from the apprehension of the great calamity foretold. It is noticeable that the popular prejudices and vulgar errors in regard to pestilences and wars—errors which were wont to prevail upon every appearance of a comet—were now altogether unknown. As if by some sudden convulsive exertion, reason had at once hurled superstition from her throne. The feeblest intellect had derived vigor from excessive interest.

What minor evils might arise from the contact were points of elaborate question. The learned spoke of slight geological disturbances, of probable alterations in climate, and consequently in vegetation, of possible magnetic and electric influences. Many held that no visible or perceptible effect would in any manner be produced. While such discussions were going on, their subject gradually approached, growing larger in apparent diameter, and of a more brilliant lustre. Mankind grew paler as it came. All human operations were suspended.

There was an epoch in the course of the general sentiment when the comet had attained, at length, a size surpassing that of any previously recorded visitation. The people now, dismissing any lingering hope that the astronomers were wrong, experienced all the certainty of evil. The chimerical aspect of their terror was gone. The hearts of the stoutest of our race beat violently within their bosoms. A very few days sufficed, however, to merge even such feelings in sentiments more unendurable We could no longer apply to the strange orb any accustomed thoughts. Its historical attributes had disappeared. It oppressed us with a hideous novelty of emotion. We saw it not as an astronomical phenomenon in the heavens, but as an incubus upon our hearts, and a shadow upon our brains. It had taken, with inconceivable rapidity, the character of a gigantic mantle of rare flame, extending from horizon to horizon.

Yet a day, and men breathed with greater freedom. It was clear that we were already within the influence of the comet; yet we lived. We even felt an unusual elasticity of frame and vivacity of mind. The exceeding tenuity of the object of our dread was apparent; for all heavenly objects were plainly visible through it. Meantime, our vegetation had perceptibly altered; and we gained faith, from this predicted circumstance, in the foresight of the wise. A wild luxuriance of foliage, utterly unknown before, burst out upon every vegetable thing.

Yet another day—and the evil was not altogether upon us. It was now evident that its nucleus would first reach us. A wild change had come over all men; and the first sense of pain was the wild signal for general lamentation and horror. This first sense of pain lay in a rigorous constriction of the breast and lungs, and an insufferable dryness of the skin. It could not be denied that our atmosphere was radically affected; the conformation of this atmosphere and the possible modifications to which it might be subjected, were now the topics of discussion. The result of investigation sent an electric thrill of the intensest terror through the universal heart of man.

It had been long known that the air which encircled us was a compound of oxygen and nitrogen gases, in the proportion of twenty–one measures of oxygen, and seventy–nine of nitrogen in every one hundred of the atmosphere. Oxygen, which was the principle of combustion, and the vehicle of heat, was absolutely necessary to the support of animal life, and was the most powerful and energetic agent in nature. Nitrogen, on the contrary, was incapable of supporting either animal life or flame. An unnatural excess of oxygen would result, it had been ascertained in just such an elevation of the animal spirits as we had latterly experienced. It was the pursuit, the extension of the idea, which had engendered awe. What would be the result of a total extraction of the nitrogen? A combustion irresistible, all–devouring, omni–prevalent, immediate;—the entire fulfilment, in all their minute and terrible details, of the fiery and horror–inspiring denunciations of the prophecies of the Holy Book.

Why need I paint, Charmion, the now disenchained frenzy of mankind? That tenuity in the comet which had previously inspired us with hope, was now the source of the bitterness of despair. In its impalpable gaseous character we clearly perceived the consummation of Fate. Meantime a day again passed—bearing away with it the last shadow of Hope. We gasped in the rapid modification of the air. The red blood bounded tumultuously through its strict channels. A furious delirium possessed all men; and, with arms rigidly outstretched towards the threatening heavens, they trembled and shrieked aloud. But the nucleus of the destroyer was now upon us; even here in Aidenn, I shudder while I speak. Let me be brief—brief as the ruin that overwhelmed. For a moment there was a wild lurid light alone, visiting and penetrating all things. Then—let us bow down, Charmion, before the excessive majesty of the great God!—then, there came a shouting and pervading sound, as if from the mouth itself of HIM; while the whole incumbent mass of ether in which we existed, burst at once into a species of intense flame, for whose surpassing brilliancy and all-fervid heat even the angels in the high Heaven of pure knowledge have no name. Thus ended all.

Edward Page Mitchell
(1852-1927)

A pioneering science fiction writer who worked as editor of *The Sun* newspaper in New York. He wrote about time travel, faster-than-light travel, and cyborgs before these became common themes, though his work was largely forgotten for many years.

The Man Without a Body
Edward Page Mitchell

On a shelf in the old Arsenal Museum, in the Central Park, in the midst of stuffed hummingbirds, ermines, silver foxes, and bright- colored parakeets, there is a ghastly row of human heads. I pass by the mummied Peruvian, the Maori chief, and the Flathead Indian to speak of a Caucasian head which has had a fascinating interest to me ever since it was added to the grim collection a little more than a year ago.

I was struck with the Head when I first saw it. The pensive intelligence of the features won me. The face is remarkable, although the nose is gone, and the nasal fossae are somewhat the worse for wear. The eyes are likewise wanting, but the empty orbs have an expression of their own. The parchmenty skin is so shriveled that the teeth show to their roots in the jaws. The mouth has been much affected by the ravages of decay, but what mouth there is displays character. It seems to say: 'Barring certain deficiencies in my anatomy, you behold a man of parts!' The features of the Head are of the Teutonic cast, and the skull is the skull of a philosopher. What particularly attracted my attention, however, was the vague resemblance which this dilapidated countenance bore to some face which had at some time been familiar to me—some face which lingered in my memory, but which I could not place.

After all, I was not greatly surprised, when I had known the Head for nearly a year, to see it acknowledge our acquaintance and express its appreciation of friendly interest on my part by deliberately winking at me as I stood before its glass case.

This was on a Trustees' Day, and I was the only visitor in the hall. The faithful attendant had gone to enjoy a can of beer with his friend, the superintendent of the monkeys.

The Head winked a second time, and even more cordially than before. I gazed upon its efforts with the critical delight of an anatomist. I saw the masseter muscle flex beneath the leathery skin. I saw the play of the glutinators, and the beautiful lateral movement of the internal playtsyma. I knew the Head was trying to speak to me. I noted the convulsive twitchings of the risorius and the zygomatie major, and knew that it was endeavoring to smile.

'Here,' I thought, 'is either a case of vitality long after decapitation, or, an instance of reflex action where there is no diastaltic or excitor-motory system. In either case the phenomenon is unprecedented, and should be carefully observed. Besides, the Head is evidently well disposed toward me.' I found a key on my bunch which opened the glass door.

'Thanks,' said the Head. 'A breath of fresh air is quite a treat.'

'How do you feel?' I asked politely. 'How does it seem without a body?'

The Head shook itself sadly and sighed. 'I would give,' it said, speaking through its ruined nose, and for obvious reasons using chest tones sparingly, 'I would give both ears for a single leg. My ambition is principally ambulatory, and yet I cannot walk. I cannot even hop or waddle. I would fain travel, roam, promenade, circulate in the busy paths of men, but I am chained to this accursed shelf. I am no better off than these barbarian heads—I, a man of science! I am compelled to sit here on my neck and see sandpipers and storks all around me, with legs and to spare. Look at that infernal little Oedieneninus longpipes over there. Look at that miserable gray–headed porphyric. They have no brains, no ambition, no yearnings. Yet they have legs, legs, legs, in profusion.' He cast an envious glance across the alcove at the tantalizing limbs of the birds in question and added gloomily, 'There isn't even enough of me to make a hero for one of Wilkie Collins's novels.'

I did not exactly know how to console him in so delicate a manner, but ventured to hint that perhaps his condition had its compensations in immunity from corns and the gout.

'And as to arms,' he went on, 'there's another misfortune for you! I am unable to brush away the flies that get in here—Lord knows how—in the summertime. I cannot reach over and cuff that confounded Chinook mummy that sits there grinning at me like a jack–in–the–box. I cannot scratch my head or even blow my nose (his nose!) decently when I get cold in this thundering draft. As to eating and drinking, I don't care. My soul is wrapped up in science. Science is my bride, my divinity. I worship her footsteps in the past and hail the prophecy of her future progress. I–'

I had heard these sentiments before. In a flash I had accounted for the familiar look which had haunted me ever since I first saw the Head. 'Pardon me,' I said, 'you are the celebrated Professor Dummkopf?'

'That is, or was, my name,' he replied, with dignity.

'And you formerly lived in Boston, where you carried on scientific experiments of startling originality. It was you who first discovered how to photograph smell, how to bottle music, how to freeze the aurora borealis. It was you who first applied spectrW analysis to Mind.'

'Those were some of my minor achievements,' said the Head, sadly nodding itself—'small when compared with my final invention, the grand discovery which was at the same time my greatest triumph and my ruin. I lost my Body in an experiment.'

'How was that?' I asked. 'I had not heard.'

'No,' said the Head. 'I being alone and friendless, my disappearance was hardly noticed. I will tell you.'

There was a sound upon the stairway. 'Hush!' cried the Head. 'Here comes somebody. We must not be discovered. You must dissemble.'

I hastily closed the door of the glass case, locking it just in time to evade the vigilance of the returning keeper, and dissembled by pretending to examine, with great interest, a nearby exhibit.

On the next Trustees' Day I revisited the museum and gave the keeper of the Head a dollar on the pretense of purchasing information in regard to the curiosities in his charge. He made the circuit of the hall with me, talking volubly all the while.

'That there,' he said, as we stood before the Head, 'is a relic of morality presented to the museum fifteen months ago. The head of a notorious murderer guillotined at Paris in the last century, sir.'

I fancied that I saw a slight twitching about the corners of Professor Dummkopf's mouth and an almost imperceptible depression of what was once his left eyelid, but he kept his face remarkably well under the circumstances. I dismissed my guide with many thanks for his intelligent services, and, as I had anticipated, he departed forthwith to invest his easily earned dollar in beer, leaving me to pursue my conversation with the Head.

'Think of putting a wooden–headed idiot like that,' said the professor, after I had opened his glass prison, 'in charge of a portion, however small, of a man of science—of the inventor of the Telepomp! Paris! Murderer! Last century, indeed!' and the Head shook with laughter until I feared that it would tumble off the shelf.

'You spoke of your invention, the Telepomp,' I suggested.

'Ah, yes,' said the Head, simultaneously recovering its gravity and its center of gravity; 'I promised to tell you how I happen to be a Man without a Body. You see that some three or four years ago I discovered the principle of the transmission of sound by electricity. My telephone, as I called it, would have been an invention of great practical utility if I had been spared to introduce it to the public. But, alas–'

'Excuse the interruption,' I said, 'but I must inform you that somebody else has recently accomplished the same thing. The telephone is a realized fact.'

'Have they gone any further?' he eagerly asked. 'Have they discovered the great secret of the transmission of atoms? In other words, have they accomplished the Telepomp?'

'I have heard nothing of the kind,' I hastened to assure him, 'but what do you mean?'

'Listen,' he said. 'In the course of my experiments with the telephone I became convinced that the same principle was capable of indefinite expansion. Matter is made up of molecules, and molecules, in their turn, are made up of atoms. The atom, you know, is the unit of being. The molecules differ according to the number and the arrangement of their constituent atoms. Chemical changes are effected by the dissolution of the atoms in the molecules and their rearrangements into molecules of another kind. This dissolution may be accomplished by chemical affinity or by a sufficiently strong electric current. Do you follow me?'

'Perfectly.'

'Well, then, following out this line of thought, I conceived a great idea. There was no reason why matter could not be telegraphed, or, to be etymologically accurate, 'telepomped.' It was only necessary to effect at one end of the line the disintegration of the molecules into atoms and to convey the vibrations of the chemical dissolution by electricity to the other pole, where a corresponding reconstruction could be effected from other atoms. As all atoms are alike, their arrangement into molecules of the same order, and the arrangement of those molecules into an organization similar to the original organization, would be practically a reproduction of the original. It would be a materialization—not in the sense of the spiritualists' cant, but in all the truth and logic of stern science. Do you still follow me?'

'It is a little misty,' I said, 'but I think I get the point. You would telegraph the Idea of the matter, to use the word Idea in Plato's sense.'

'Precisely. A candle flame is the same candle flame although the burning gas is continually changing. A wave on the surface of water is the same wave, although the water composing it is shifting as it moves. A man is the same man although there is not an atom in his body which was there five years before. It is the form, the shape, the Idea, that is essential. The vibrations that give individuality to matter may be transmitted to a distance by wire just as readily as the vibrations that give individuality to sound. So I constructed an instrument by which I could pull down matter, so to speak, at the anode and build it up again on the same plan at the cathode. This was my Telepomp.'

'But in practice—how did the Telepomp work?'

'To perfection! In my rooms on joy Street, in Boston, I had about five miles of wire. I had no difficulty in sending simple compounds, such as quartz, starch, and water, from one room to another over this five–mile coil. I shall never forget the joy with which I disintegrated a three–cent postage stamp in one room and found it immediately reproduced at the receiving instrument in another. This success with inorganic matter emboldened me to attempt the same thing with a living organism. I caught a cat—a black and yellow cat—and I submitted him to a terrible current from my two–hundred–cup battery. The cat disappeared in a twinkling. I hastened to the next room and, to my immense satisfaction, found Thomas there, alive and purring, although somewhat astonished. It worked like a charm.'

'This is certainly very remarkable.'

'Isn't it? After my experiment with the cat, a gigantic idea took possession of me. If I could send a feline being, why not send a human being? If I could transmit a cat five miles by wire in an instant by electricity, why not transmit a man to London by Atlantic cable and with equal dispatch? I resolved to strengthen my already powerful battery and try the experiment. Like a thorough votary of science, I resolved to try the experiment on myself.

'I do not like to dwell upon this chapter of my experience,' continued the Head, winking at a tear which had trickled down on to his cheek and which I gently wiped away for him with my own pocket handkerchief. 'Suffice it that I trebled the cups in my battery, stretched my wire over housetops to my lodgings in Phillips Street, made everything ready, and with a solemn calmness born of my confidence in the theory, placed myself in the receiving instrument of the Telepomp at my Joy Street office. I was as sure that when I made the connection with the battery I would find myself in my rooms in Phillips Street as I was sure of my existence. Then I touched the key that let on the electricity. Alas!'

For some moments my friend was unable to speak. At last, with an effort, he resumed his narrative.

'I began to disintegrate at my feet and slowly disappeared under my own eyes. My legs melted away, and then my trunk and arms. That something was wrong,

I knew from the exceeding slowness of my dissolution, but I was helpless. Then my head went and I lost all consciousness. According to my theory, my head, having been the last to disappear, should have been the first to materialize at the other end of the wire. The theory was confirmed in fact. I recovered consciousness. I opened my eyes in my Phillips Street apartments. My chin was materializing, and with great satisfaction I saw my neck slowly taking shape. Suddenly, and about at the third cervical vertebra, the process stopped. In a flash I knew the reason. I had forgotten to replenish the cups of my battery with fresh sulphuric acid, and there was not electricity enough to materialize the rest of me. I was a Head, but my body was Lord knows where.'

I did not attempt to offer consolation. Words would have been mockery in the presence of Professor Dummkopf's grief.

'What matters it about the rest?' he sadly continued. 'The house in Phillips Street was full of medical students. I suppose that some of them found my head, and knowing nothing of me or of the Telepomp, appropriated it for purposes of anatomical study. I suppose that they attempted to preserve it by means of some arsenical preparation. How badly the work was done is shown by my defective nose. I suppose that I drifted from medical student to medical student and from anatomical cabinet to anatomical cabinet until some would–be humorist presented me to this collection as a French murderer of the last century. For some months I knew nothing, and when I recovered consciousness I found myself here.

'Such,' added the Head, with a dry, harsh laugh, 'is the irony of fate!'

'Is there nothing I can do for you?' I asked, after a pause.

'Thank you,' the Head replied; 'I am tolerably cheerful and resigned. I have lost pretty much all interest in experimental science. I sit here day after day and watch the objects of zoological, ichthyological, ethnological, and conchological interest with which this admirable museum abounds. I don't know of anything you can do for me.

'Stay,' he added, as his gaze fell once more upon the exasperating legs of the Oedienenius longpipes opposite him. 'If there is anything I do feel the need of, it is outdoor exercise. Couldn't you manage in some way to take me out for a walk?'

I confess that I was somewhat staggered by this request, but promised to do what I could. After some deliberation, I formed a plan, which was carried out in the following manner:

I returned to the museum that afternoon just before the closing hour, and hid myself behind the mammoth sea cow, or Manatus Americanus. The attendant, after a cursory glance through the hall, locked up the building and departed. Then I came boldly forth and removed my friend from his shelf. With a piece of stout twine, I lashed his one or two vertebrae to the headless vertebrae of a skeleton moa. This gigantic and extinct bird of New Zealand is heavy–legged, full–breasted, tall as a man, and has huge, sprawling feet. My friend, thus provided with legs and arms, manifested extraordinary glee. He walked about, stamped his big feet, swung his wings, and occasionally broke forth into a hilarious shuffle. I was obliged to remind him that he must support the dignity of the venerable bird whose skeleton he had borrowed. I despoiled the African lion of his glass eyes, and inserted them in the empty orbits of the Head. I gave Professor Dummkopf a Fiji war lance for a walking stick, covered him with a Sioux blanket, and then we issued forth from the old arsenal into the fresh night air and the moonlight, and wandered arm in arm along the shores of the quiet lake and through the mazy paths of the Ramble.

H G Wells
(1866-1946)

Helped establish science fiction as a serious genre with classics like *The Time Machine, The War of the Worlds,* and *The Invisible Man.* Beyond writing, he was a prominent social commentator who advocated for human rights and predicted many modern developments.

The Star

H G Wells

It was on the first day of the new year that the announcement was made, almost simultaneously from three observatories, that the motion of the planet Neptune, the outermost of all the planets that wheeled about the sun, had become erratic. Ogilvy had already called attention to a suspected retardation in its velocity in December. Such a piece of news was scarcely calculated to interest the world the greater portion of whose inhabitants were unaware of the existence of the planet Neptune, nor outside the astronomical profession did the subsequent discovery of a faint remote speck of light in the region of the perturbed planet cause any great excitement.

Scientific people, however, found the intelligence remarkable enough, even before it became known that the new body was rapidly growing larger and brighter, that its motion was quite different from the orderly progress of the planets, and that the deflection of Neptune and its satellite was becoming now of an unprecedented kind.

Few people without training in science can realize the huge isolation of the solar system. The sun with its specks of planets, its dust of planetoids, and its impalpable comets swims in vacant immensity that almost defeats the imagination. Beyond the orbit of Neptune there is space, vacant so far as human observation has penetrated, without warmth or light or sound, blank emptiness, for twenty billion times a million miles. That is the smallest estimate of the distance to be traversed before the nearest of the stars is attained. And, saving a few comets, more unsubstantial than the thinnest flame, no matter had ever to human knowledge crossed the gulf of space, until early in the twentieth century this wanderer appeared.

A vast mass of matter it was, bulky, heavy, rushing without warning out of the black mystery of the sky into the radiance of the sun. By the second day it was clearly visible to any decent instrument, as a speck with a barely sensible diameter, in the constellation Leo near Regulus. In a little while an opera glass could attain it.

On the third day of the new year the newspaper readers of two hemispheres were made aware for the first time of the real importance of this unusual apparition in the heavens. 'A Planetary Collision,' one London paper headed the news, and proclaimed Duchine's opinion that this strange new planet would probably collide with

Neptune. The leader writers enlarged upon the topic. So that in most of the capitals of the world, on Jan. 3, there was an expectation, however vague, of some eminent phenomenon in the sky; and as the night followed the sunset round the globe thousands of men turned their eyes skyward to see—the old familiar stars just as they had always been.

Until it was dawn in London and Pollux setting, and the stars overhead grown pale. The winter's dawn it was, a sickly filtering accumulation of daylight, and the light of gas and candles shone yellow in the windows to show where people were astir. But the yawning policeman saw the thing, the busy crowds in the market stopped agape, workmen going to their work betimes, milkmen, the drivers of news carts, dissipation going home jaded and pale, homeless wanderers, sentinels on their beats, and in the country, laborers trudging afield, poachers slinking home, all over the dusky quickening country it would be seen—and out at sea by seamen watching for the day—a great white star, come suddenly into the westward sky!

Brighter it was than any star in our skies; brighter than the evening star at its brightest. It still glowed out white and large, no mere twinkling spot of light but a small round clear shining disk, an hour after the day had come. And where science has not reached, men stared and feared, telling one another of the wars and pestilences that are foreshadowed by these fiery signs in the heavens.

Sturdy Boers, dusky Hottentots, Gold Coast negroes, Frenchmen, Spaniards, Portuguese, stood in the glow of the sunrise watching the setting of this strange new star.

And in a hundred observatories there had been suppressed excitement, rising almost to shouting pitch, as the two remote bodies had rushed together. There had been a hurrying to and fro to gather photographic apparatus and spectroscope; to gather this appliance and that, to record the novel astonishing sight, the destruction of a world,—for it was a world, a sister planet of our earth, far greater than our earth indeed, that had so suddenly flashed into flaming death. Neptune it was, which had been struck, fairly, and squarely, by the planet from outer space and the heat of concussion had incontinently turned two solid globes into one vast mass of incandescence.

Round the world that day, two hours before the dawn, went the pallid great white star, fading only as it sank westward and the sun mounted above it. Everywhere man marveled at it, but of all those who saw it none could have marveled more than those sailors, habitual watchers of the stars, who far away at sea had heard nothing of its advent and saw it now rise like a pigmy moon and climb zenithward and hang overhead and sink westward with the passing of the night.

And when next it rose over Europe everywhere were crowds of watchers on hilly slopes, on house roofs, in open spaces, staring eastward, waiting for the rising of the new star. It rose with a white glow in front, like the glare of a white fire, and those who had seen it come into existence the night before cried out at the sight of it. 'It is larger,' they cried. 'It is brighter!' And, indeed, the moon a quarter full and sinking in the west was in its apparent size beyond comparison, but scarcely in all its breadth had it as much brightness now as the little circle of the strange new star.

'It is brighter!' cried the people clustering in the streets. But in the dim observatories the watchers held their breath and peered at one another. 'It is nearer,' they said. 'Nearer!'

And voice after voice repeated. 'It is nearer,' and the clicking telegraph took that up, and it trembled along telephone wires, and in a thousand cities grimy compositors fingered the type. 'It is nearer.' Men writing in offices, struck with strange realization, flung down their pens, men talking in a thousand places suddenly came upon a grotesque possibility in those words, 'It is nearer.' It hurried along awakening streets, it was shouted down the frost–stilled ways of quiet villages, men who had read these things, from the throbbing tape stood in yellow–lit doorways shouting the news to the passers–by. 'It is nearer.' Pretty women flushed and glittering, heard the news told jestingly between dances, and feigned an intelligent interest they did not feel. 'Nearer! Indeed. How curious! How clever people must be to find out things like that!'

Lonely tramps faring through the wintry night murmured those words to comfort themselves—looking skyward. 'It has need to be nearer, for the night's as cold as charity. Don't seem much warmth from it if it is nearer, all the same.'

'What is a new star to me?' cried the weeping woman kneeling beside her dead.

The schoolboy, rising early for his examination work, puzzled it out for himself—with the great white star shining broad and bright through the frost–flowers of his window. 'Centrifugal, centripetal,' he said, with his chin on his fist. 'Stop a planet in its flight, rob it of its centrifugal force, what then? Centripetal has it, and down it falls into the sun! And this——!'

'Do we come in the way? I wonder——'

The light of that day went the way of its brethren, and with the later watches of the frosty darkness rose the strange star again, And it was now so bright that the waxing moon seemed but a pale yellow ghost of itself, rising huge in the sunset hour. In a South African city a great man had married, and the streets were alight to welcome his return with his bride. 'Even the skies have illuminated,' said the flatterer. Under Capricorn, two negro lovers, daring the wild beasts and evil spirits, for love of one another, crouched together in a cane brake where the fireflies hovered. 'That is our star,' they whispered, and felt strangely comforted by the sweet brilliancy of its light.

The master mathematician sat in his private room and pushed the papers from him. His calculations were already finished. In a small white phial there still remained a little of the drug that had kept him awake and active for four long nights. Each day, serene, explicit, patient as ever, he had given his lecture to his students, and then had come back at once to his momentous calculation. His face was grave, a little drawn, and hectic from his drugged activity. For some time he seemed lost in thought. Then he went to the window, and the blind went up with a click. Half way up the sky, over the clustering roofs, chimneys, and steeples of the city, hung the star.

He looked at it as one might look into the eye of a brave enemy. 'You may kill me,' he said after a silence, 'But I can hold you—and all the universe for that matter—in the grip of this little brain. I would not change even now.'

He looked at the little phial. 'There will be no need of sleep again,' he said. The next day at noon, punctual to the minute, he entered his lecture theater, put his hat on the end of the table as his habit was, and carefully selected a large piece of chalk. It was a joke among his students that he could not lecture without that piece of chalk to fumble in his fingers, and once he had been stricken to impotence by their hiding his supply. He came and looked under his gray eyebrows at the rising tiers of young fresh faces, and spoke with his accustomed studied commonness of phrasing, 'Circumstances have arisen—circumstances beyond my control,' he said and paused, 'which will debar me from completing the course I had designed. It would seem, gentlemen, if I may put the thing clearly and briefly, that—man has lived in vain.'

The students glanced at one another. Had they heard aright? Mad? Raised eyebrows and grinning lips there were, but one or two faces remained intent upon his calm gray–fringed face. 'It will be interesting,' he was saying, 'to devote this morning to an exposition, so far as I can make it clear to you, of the calculations that have led me to this conclusion. Let us assume——'

He turned toward the blackboard, meditating a diagram in the way that was usual to him. 'What was that about 'lived in vain'?' whispered one student to another. 'Listen,' said the other, nodding toward the lecturer.

And presently they began to understand.

That night the star rose later, for its proper eastward motion had carried it some way across Leo toward Virgo, and its brightness was so great that the sky became a luminous blue as it rose, and every star and planet was hidden, save only Jupiter near the zenith, Capella, Aldebaran, Sirius, and the pointers of the Bear. It was white and beautiful. In many parts of the world that night a pallid halo encircled it about. It was perceptibly larger; in the clear refractive sky of the tropics it seemed as if it were nearly a quarter of the size of the moon. The frost was still on the ground in England, but the world was as brightly lit as if it were midsummer moonlight. One could see to read quite ordinary print by that cold clear light, and in the cities the lamps burnt yellow and wan.

And everywhere the world was awake that night, and throughout Christendom a somber murmur hung in the keen air over the countryside like the buzzing of the bees in the heather, and this murmurous tumult grew to a clangor in the cities. It was the tolling of the bells in a million belfry towers and steeples, summoning the people to sleep no more, to sin no more, but to gather in their churches and pray. And overhead, growing larger and brighter, as the earth rolled on its way and the night passed, rose the dazzling star.

And the streets and houses were alight in all the cities, the shipyards glared, and whatever roads led to high country were lit and crowded all night long. And in all the seas about the civilized lands ships with throbbing engines, and ships with bellying sails, crowded with men and living creatures, were standing out to ocean and the north. For already the warning of the master mathematician had been telegraphed over the world, and translated into a hundred tongues. The new planet and Neptune, locked in a fiery embrace, were whirling headlong, ever faster and faster, toward the sun. Already every second this blazing mass flew a hundred miles, and every second its terrific velocity increased. As it flew its course, it must pass a hundred million of miles wide of the earth and scarcely affect it.

But near its destined path, as yet only slightly perturbed, spun the mighty planet Jupiter and his moons sweeping splendid around the sun. Every moment now the attraction between the fiery star and the greatest of the planets grew stronger. And the result of that attraction? Inevitably Jupiter, would be deflected from its orbit to a new elliptical path, and the burning star, swung by his attraction wide of its sunward rush, would 'describe a curved path' and perhaps collide with and certainly pass close to, our earth. 'Earthquakes, volcanic outbreaks, cyclones, sea waves, floods, and a steady rise in temperature to I know not what limit'—so prophesied the master mathematician.

And overhead, to carry out his words, lonely and cold and livid, blazed the star of the coming doom.

To many who stared at it that night until their eyes ached, it seemed that it was visibly approaching. And that night, too, the weather changed, and the frost that had gripped all Central Europe and France and England softened towards a thaw.

But you must not imagine because I have spoken of people praying through the night and people going aboard ships and people fleeing towards mountainous country that the whole world was already in a terror because of the star. As a matter of fact, use and wont still ruled the world, and save for the talk of idle moments and the splendor of the night, nine human beings out of ten were still busy at their common occupations. In all the cities the shops, save one here and there, opened and closed at their proper hours, the doctor and the undertaker plied their trades, and workers gathered in the factories, soldiers drilled, scholars studied, lovers sought one another, thieves lurked and fled, politicians planned their schemes. The presses of the newspapers roared through the nights, and many a priest of this church and that would not open his holy building to further what he considered a foolish panic.

The newspapers insisted on the lesson of the year 1000—for then, too, people had anticipated the end. The star was no star—mere gas—a comet; and were it a star it could not possibly strike the earth. There was no precedent for such a thing. Common sense was sturdy everywhere, scornful, jesting, a little inclined to persecute the obdurate fearful. That night at 7:15 by Greenwich time the star would be at its nearest to Jupiter. Then the world would see the turn things would take. The master mathematician's grim warnings were treated by many as so much mere elaborate self–advertisement. Common sense at last, a little heated by argument, signified its unalterable convictions by going to bed. So, too, barbarism and savagery, already tired of the novelty, went about their nightly business: and save for a howling dog here and there the beast–world left the star unheeded.

And yet, when at last the watchers in the European states saw their star rise, an hour later, it is true, but no larger than it had been the night before, there were still plenty awake to laugh at the master mathematician—to take the danger as if it had passed.

But hereafter the laughter ceased. The star grew—it grew with a terrible steadiness hour after hour, a little larger each hour, a little nearer the midnight zenith, and brighter and brighter, until it had turned night into day. Had it come straight to the earth instead of in a curved path, had it lost no velocity to Jupiter, it must have leapt the intervening gulf in a day; but as it was it took five days altogether to come by our planet. The next night it had become a third the size of the moon before it set to English eyes, and the thaw was assured.

It rose over America nearly the size of the moon, but blinding white to look at, and hot; and a breath of hot wind blew now with its rising and gathering strength, and in Virginia and Brazil and down the St. Lawrence valley it shone intermittently through a driving reek of thunder clouds, flickering violet lightning, and hail unprecedented. In Manitoba were a thaw and devastating floods. And upon the mountains of the earth the snow and ice began to melt that night, and all the rivers coming out of high country flowed thick and turbid, and soon—in their upper reaches—with swirling trees and the bodies of beasts and men. They rose steadily, steadily in the ghostly brilliance, and came trickling over their banks at last, behind the flying population of their valleys.

And along the coast of Argentina and up the South Atlantic tides were higher than they had ever been in the memory of man, and the storms drove the waters in many cases scores of miles inland, drowning whole cities. And so great grew the heat during the night that the rising of the sun was like the coming of a shadow. The earthquakes began and grew until all down America from the Arctic Circle to Cape Horn hillsides were sliding, fissures were opening, and houses and walls crumbling to destruction.

China was lit glowing white, but over Japan and Java and all the islands of eastern Asia the great star was a ball of dull red fire because of the steam and smoke and ashes the volcanoes were spouting forth to salute its coming. Above were the lava, hot gases, and ash, and below the seething floods, and the whole earth swayed and rumbled with the earthquake shocks. Soon the immemorial snows of Tibet and the Himalayas were melting and pouring down by ten million deepening converging channels upon the plains of Burma and Hindustan. The tangled summits of the Indian jungles were aflame in a thousand places, and below the hurrying waters around the stems were dark objects that struggled feebly and reflected the blood red tongues of fire. And in a ungovernable confusion a multitude of men and women fled down the broad riverways to that one last hope of men—the open sea.

Larger grew the star, and larger, hotter, and brighter with a terrible swiftness now. The tropical ocean had lost its phosphorescence, and the whirling steam rose in ghostly wreaths from the black waves that plunged incessantly, speckled with storm–tossed ships.

And then came a wonder. It seemed to those who in Europe watched for the rising of the star that the world must have ceased its rotation. In a thousand open spaces of down and upland the people who had fled thither from the floods and the falling houses and sliding slopes of hill watched for that rising in vain. Hour followed hour through a terrible suspense, and the star rose not. Once again men set their eyes upon the old constellations they had counted lost to them forever. In England it was hot and clear overhead, though the ground quivered perpetually; but in the tropics Sirius and Capella and Aldebaran showed through a veil of steam. And when at last the great star rose, near ten hours late, the sun rose close upon it, and in the center of its white heart was a disk of black.

Over Asia the star had begun to fall behind the movement of the sky, and then suddenly, as it hung over India, its light had been veiled. All the plain of India from the mouth of the Indus to the mouths of the Ganges was a shallow waste of shining water that night, out of which rose temples and palaces, mounds and hills, black with people. Every minaret was a clustering mass of people, who fell one by one into the turbid waters as heat and terror overcame them. The whole land seemed a–wailing, and suddenly there swept a shadow across that furnace of despair, and a breath of cold wind, and a gathering of clouds out of the cooling air. Men looking up, nearly blinded, at the star, and saw that black disk creeping across the light. It was the moon, coming between the star and the earth. And even as men cried to God at this respite, out of the east with a strange, inexplicable swiftness sprang the sun. And then star, sun, and moon rushed together across the heavens.

So it was that presently, to the European watchers, star and sun rose close upon each other, drove headlong for a space, and then slower, and at last came to rest, star and sun merged into one glare of flame at the zenith of the sky. The moon no longer eclipsed the star, but was lost to sight in the brilliance of the sky. And though those who were still alive regarded it for the most part with that dull stupidity that hunger, fatigue, heat, and despair engender, there were still men who could perceive the meaning of these signs. Star and earth had been at their nearest, had swung about one another, and the star had passed. Already it was receding, swifter and swifter, in the last stage of its headlong journey downward into the sun.

And then the clouds gathered, blotting out the vision of the sky; the thunder and lightning wove a garment around the world; all over the earth was such a downpour of rain as men had never seen before; and where the volcanoes flared red against the cloud canopy there descended torrents of mud. Everywhere the waters were pouring off the land, leaving mud stilted ruins, and the earth littered like a storm–worn beach with all that had floated, and the dead bodies of the men and brutes, its children.

For days the water streamed off the land, sweeping away soil and trees and houses in the way and piling huge dikes and scooping out titanic gullies over the countryside. Those were the days of darkness that followed the star and the heat. All through them, and for many weeks and months, the earthquakes continued.

But the star had passed, and men, hunger–driven and gathering courage only slowly, might creep back to their ruined cities, buried granaries, and sodden fields. Such few ships as had escaped the storms of that time came stunned and shattered and sounding their way cautiously through the new marks and shoals of once familiar ports. And as the storms subsided men perceived that everywhere the days were hotter than of yore, and the sun larger, and the moon, shrunk to a third of its size, took now fourscore days between its new and new.

But of the new brotherhood that grew presently among men, of the saving of laws and machines, of the strange change that had Iceland and Greenland the shores of Baffin's Bay, so that the sailors coming there presently found them green and gracious, and could scarce believe their eyes, this story does not tell. Nor of the movement of mankind, now that the earth was hotter, northward and southward towards the poles of the earth. It concerns itself only with the coming and the passing of the star.

The Martian astronomers—for there are astronomers

on Mars, although they are different beings from men—were naturally profoundly interested by these things. They saw them from their own standpoint, of course. 'Considering the mass and temperature of the missile that was flung through our solar system into the sun,' one wrote, 'it is astonishing what little damage the earth, which it missed so narrowly, has sustained. All the familiar continental markings and the masses of the seas remain intact, and indeed the only difference seems to be a shrinkage of the white discoloration (supposed to be frozen water) round either pole.' Which only shows how small the vastest of human catastrophies may seem at a distance of a few million miles.

Aldous Huxley
(1894-1963)

Wrote the influential dystopian novel *Brave New World* and later works about psychedelic experiences like *The Doors of Perception.* He came from a famous scientific family and later moved to California, where he explored mysticism and consciousness.

The Gioconda Smile

Aldous Huxley

I

'Miss Spence will be down directly, sir.'

'Thank you,' said Mr Hutton, without turning round. Janet Spence's parlourmaid was so ugly—ugly on purpose, it always seemed to him, malignantly, criminally ugly—that he could not bear to look at her more than was necessary. The door closed. Left to himself, Mr Hutton got up and began to wander round the room, looking with meditative eyes at the familiar objects it contained.

Photographs of Greek statuary, photographs of the Roman Forum, coloured prints of Italian masterpieces, all very safe and well known. Poor, dear Janet, what a prig—what an intellectual snob! Her real taste was illustrated in that water-colour by the pavement artist, the one she had paid half a crown for (and thirty–five shillings for the frame). How often his had heard her tell the story, how often expatiate on the beauties of that skilful imitation of an oleograph! 'A real Artist in the streets,' and you could hear the capital A in Artist as she spoke the words. She made you feel that part of his glory had entered into Janet Spence when she tendered him that half–crown for the copy of the oleograph. She was implying a compliment to her own taste and penetration. A genuine Old Master for half a crown. Poor, dear Janet!

Mr Hutton came to a pause in front of a small oblong mirror. Stooping a little to get a full view of his face, he passed a white, well–manicured finger over his moustache. It was as curly, as freshly auburn as it had been twenty years ago. His hair still retained its colour, and there was no sign of baldness yet—only a certain elevation of the brow. 'Shakespearean,' thought Mr Hutton, with a smile, as he surveyed the smooth and polished expanse of his forehead.

Others abide our question, thou art free.... Footsteps in the sea ... Majesty ... Shakespeare, thou shouldst be living at this hour. No, that was Milton, wasn't it? Milton, the Lady of Christ's. There was no lady about him. He was what the women, would call a manly man. That was why they liked him—for the curly auburn moustache and the discreet redolence of tobacco. Mr Hutton smiled again; he enjoyed making fun of himself. Lady of Christ's? No, no. He was the Christ of Ladies. Very pretty, very pretty. The Christ of Ladies. Mr Hutton wished there were somebody he could tell the joke to. Poor, dear Janet wouldn't appreciate it, alas?

He straightened himself up, patted his hair, and resumed his peregrination. Damn the Roman Forum; he hated those dreary photographs.

Suddenly he became aware that Janet Spence was in the room, standing near the door. Mr Hutton started, as though he had been taken in some felonious act. To make these silent and spectral appearances was one of Janet Spence's peculiar talents. Perhaps she had been there all the time, had seen him looking at himself in the mirror. Impossible! But, still, it was disquieting.

'Oh, you gave me such a surprise,' said Mr Hutton, recovering his smile and advancing with outstretched hand to meet her.

Miss Spence was smiling too: her Gioconda smile, he had once called it, in a moment of half–ironical flattery. Miss Spence had taken the compliment seriously, and had always tried to live up to the Leonardo standard. She smiled on his silence while Mr Hutton shook hands; that was part of the Gioconda business.

'I hope you're well,' said Mr Hutton. 'You look it.'

What a queer face she had! That small mouth pursed forward by the Gioconda expression into a little snout with a round hole in the middle as though for whistling—it was like a penholder seen from the front. Above the mouth a well–shaped nose, finely aquiline. Eyes large, lustrous, and dark, with the largeness, lustre, and darkness that seems to invite sties and an occasional blood-shot suffusion. They were fine eyes, but unchangingly grave. The penholder might do its Gioconda trick, but the eyes never altered in their earnestness. Above them, a pair of boldly arched, heavily pencilled black eyebrows lent a surprising air of power, as of a Roman matron, to the upper portion of the face. Her hair was dark and equally Roman; Agrippina from the brows upward.

'I thought I'd just look in on my way home,' Mr Hutton went on. 'Ah, it's good to be back here'—he indicated with a wave of his hand the flowers in the vases, the sunshine and greenery beyond the windows —'it's good to be back in the country after a stuffy day of business in town.'

Miss Spence, who had sat down, pointed to a chair at her side.

'No, really, I cant sit down,' Mr Hutton protested. 'I must get back to see how poor Emily is. She was rather seedy this morning.' He sat down, nevertheless. 'It's these wretched liver chills. She's always getting them. Women—' He broke off and coughed, so as to hide the fact that he had uttered. He was about to say that women with weak digestions ought not to marry; but the remark was too cruel, and he didn't really believe it. Janet Spence, moreover, was a believer in eternal flames and spiritual attachments. 'She hopes to be well enough,' he added, 'to see you at luncheon to-morrow. Can you come? Do!' He smiled persuasively. 'It's my invitation too, you know.'

She dropped her eyes, and Mr Hutton almost thought

that he detected a certain reddening of the cheek. It was a tribute; he stroked his moustache.

'I should like to come if you think Emily's really well enough to have a visitor.'

'Of course. You'll do her good. You'll do us both good. In married life three is often better company than two.'

'Oh, you're cynical.'

Mr Hutton always had a desire to say 'Bow–wow–wow' whenever that last word was spoken. It irritated him more than any other word in the language. But instead of barking he made haste to protest.

'No, no. I'm only speaking a melancholy truth. Reality doesn't always come up to the ideal, you know. But that doesn't make me believe any the less in the ideal. Indeed, I believe in it passionately the ideal of a matrimony between two people in perfect accord. I think it's realisable. I'm sure it is.'

He paused significantly and looked at her with an arch expression. A virgin of thirty–six, but still unwithered; she had her charms. And there was something really rather enigmatic about her. Miss Spence made no reply but continued to smile. There were times when Mr Hutton got rather bored with the Gioconda. He stood up.

'I must really be going now. Farewell, mysterious Gioconda.' The smile grew intenser, focused itself, as it were, in a narrower snout. Mr Hutton made a Cinquecento gesture, and kissed her extended hand. It was the first time he had done such a thing; the action seemed not to be resented. 'I look forward to tomorrow.'

'Do you?'

For answer Mr Hutton once more kissed her hand, then turned to go. Miss Spence accompanied him to the porch.

'Where's your car?' she asked.

'I left it at the gate of the drive.'

'I'll come and see you off.'

'No, no.' Mr Hutton was playful, but determined. 'You must do no such thing. I simply forbid you.'

'But I should like to come,' Miss Spence protested, throwing a rapid Gioconda at him.

Mr Hutton held up his hand. 'No,' he repeated, and then, with a gesture that was almost the blowing of a kiss, he started to run down the drive, lightly on his toes, with long, bounding strides like a boy's. He was proud of that run; it was quite marvellously youthful. Still, he was glad the drive was no longer. At the last bend, before passing out of sight of the house, he halted and turned round. Miss Spence was still standing on the steps, smiling her smile. He waved his hand, and this time quite definitely and overtly wafted a kiss in her direction. Then, breaking once more into his magnificent canter, he rounded the last dark promontory of trees. Once out of sight of the house he let his high paces decline to a trot, and finally to a walk. He took out his handkerchief and began wiping his neck inside his collar. What fools, what fools! Had there ever been such an ass as poor, dear Janet Spence? Never, unless it was himself. Decidedly he was the more malignant fool, since he, at least, was aware of his folly and still persisted in it. Why did he persist? Ah, the problem that was himself, the problem that was other people.

He had reached the gate. A large, prosperous–looking motor was standing at the side of the road.

'Home, M'Nab.' The chauffeur touched his cap. 'And stop at the cross–roads on the way, as usual,' Mr Hutton added, as he opened the door of the car. 'Well?' he said, speaking into the obscurity that lurked within.

'Oh, Teddy Bear, what an age you've been!' It was a fresh and childish voice that spoke the words. There was the faintest hint of Cockney impurity about the vowel sounds.

Mr Hutton bent his large form and darted into the car with the agility of an animal regaining its burrow.

'Have I?' he said, as he shut the door. The machine began to move. 'You must have missed me a lot if you found the time so long.' He sat back in the low seat; a cherishing warmth enveloped him.

'Teddy Bear....' and with a sigh of contentment a charming little head declined on to Mr Hutton's shoulder. Ravished, he looked down sideways at the round, babyish face.

'Do you know, Doris, you look like the pictures of Louise de Kerouaille.' He passed his fingers through a mass of curly hair.

'Who's Louise de Kera–whatever–it–is?' Doris spoke from remote distances.

'She was, alas! Fuit. We shall all be 'was' one of these days. Meanwhile....'

Mr Hutton covered the babyish face with kisses. The car rushed smoothly along. McNab's back, through the front window was stonily impassive, the back of a statue.

'Your hands,' Doris whispered. 'Oh, you mustn't touch me. They give me electric shocks.'

Mr Hutton adored her for the virgin imbecility of the words. How late in one's existence one makes the discovery of one's body!

'The electricity isn't in me, it's in you.' He kissed her again, whispering her name several times: Doris, Doris, Doris. The scientific appellation of the sea–mouse, he was thinking as he kissed the throat, she offered him, white and extended like the throat of a victim awaiting the sacrificial knife. The sea–mouse was a sausage with iridescent fur: very peculiar. Or was Doris the sea cucumber, which turns itself inside out in moments of alarm? He would really have to go to Naples again, just to see the aquarium. These sea creatures were fabulous, unbelievably fantastic.

'Oh, Teddy Bear!' (More zoology; but he was only a land animal. His poor little jokes!) 'Teddy Bear, I'm so happy.'

'So am I,' said Mr Hutton. Was it true?

'But I wish I knew if it were right. Tell me, Teddy Bear, is it right or wrong?'

'Ah, my dear, that's just what I've been wondering for the last thirty years.'

'Be serious, Teddy Bear. I want to know if this is right; if it's right that I should be here with you and that we should love one another, and that it should give me electric shocks when you touch me.'

'Right? Well, it's certainly good that you should have electric shocks rather than sexual repressions. Read Freud; repressions are the devil.'

'Oh, you don't help me. Why aren't you ever serious? If only you knew how miserable I am sometimes, thinking it's not right. Perhaps, you know, there is a hell, and all that. I don t know what to do. Sometimes I think I ought to stop loving you.'

'But could you?' asked Mr Hutton, confident in the powers of his seduction and his moustache.

'No, Teddy Bear, you know I couldn't. But I could run away, I could hide from you, I could lock myself up and force myself not to come to you.'

'Silly little thing!' He tightened his embrace.

'Oh, dear, I hope it isn't wrong. And there are times when I don't care if it is.'

Mr Hutton was touched. He had a certain protective affection for this little creature. He laid his cheek against her hair and so, interlaced, they sat in silence, while the car, swaying and pitching a little as it hastened along, seemed to draw in the white road and the dusty hedges towards it devouringly.

'Good–bye, good–bye.'

The car moved on, gathered speed, vanished round a curve, and Doris was left standing by the sign–post at the cross–roads, still dizzy and weak with the languor born of those kisses and the electrical touch of those gentle hands. She had to take a deep breath, to draw herself up deliberately, before she was strong enough to start her homeward walk. She had half a mile in which to invent the necessary lies.

Alone, Mr Hutton suddenly found himself the prey of an appalling boredom.

II

Mrs Hutton was lying on the sofa in her boudoir, playing Patience. In spite of the warmth of the July evening a wood fire was burning on the hearth. A black Pomeranian, extenuated by the heat and the fatigues of digestion, slept before the blaze.

'Phew! Isn't it rather hot in here?' Mr Hutton asked as he entered the room.

'You know I have to keep warm, dear.' The voice seemed breaking on the verge of tears. 'I get so shivery.'

'I hope you're better this evening.'

'Not much, I'm afraid.'

The conversation stagnated. Mr Hutton stood leaning his back against the mantelpiece. He looked down at the Pomeranian lying at his feet, and with the toe of his right boot he rolled the little dog over and rubbed its white-flecked chest and belly. The creature lay in an inert ecstasy. Mrs Hutton continued to play Patience. Arrived at an impasse, she altered the position of one card, took back another, and went on playing. Her Patiences always came out.

'Dr Libbard thinks I ought to go to Llandrindod Wells this summer.'

'Well—go, my dear—go, most certainly.'

Mr Hutton was thinking of the events of the afternoon: how they had driven, Doris and he, up to the hanging wood, had left the car to wait for them under the shade of the trees, and walked together out into the windless sunshine of the chalk down.

'I'm to drink the waters for my liver, and he thinks I ought to have massage and electric treatment, too.'

Hat in hand, Doris had stalked four blue butterflies that were dancing together round a scabious flower with a motion that was like the flickering of blue fire. The blue fire burst and scattered into whirling sparks; she had given chase, laughing and shouting like a child.

'I'm sure it will do you good, my dear.'

'I was wondering if you'd come with me, dear.'

'But you know I'm going to Scotland at the end of the month.'

Mrs Hutton looked up at him entreatingly. 'It's the

journey,' she said. 'The thought of it is such a nightmare. I don't know if I can manage it. And you know I can't sleep in hotels. And then there's the luggage and all the worries. I can't go alone.

'But you won't be alone. You'll have your maid with you.' He spoke impatiently. The sick woman was usurping the place of the healthy one. He was being dragged back from the memory of the sunlit down and the quick, laughing girl, back to this unhealthy, overheated room and its complaining occupant.

'I don't think I shall be able to go.'

'But you must, my dear, if the doctor tells you to. And, besides, a change will do you good.'

'I don't think so.'

'But Libbard thinks so, and he knows what he's talking about.'

'No, I can't face it. I'm too weak. I can't go alone.' Mrs Hutton pulled a handkerchief out of her black silk bag, and put it to her eyes.

'Nonsense, my dear, you must make the effort.'

'I had rather be left in peace to die here.' She was crying in earnest now.

'O Lord! Now do be reasonable. Listen now, please.' Mrs Hutton only sobbed more violently. 'Oh, what is one to do?' He shrugged his shoulders and walked out of the room.

Mr Hutton was aware that he had not behaved with

proper patience; but he could not help it. Very early in his manhood he had discovered that not only did he not feel sympathy for the poor, the weak, the diseased, and deformed; he actually hated them. Once, as an undergraduate, he spent three days at a mission in the East End. He had returned, filled with a profound and ineradicable disgust. Instead of pitying, he loathed the unfortunate. It was not, he knew, a very comely emotion; and he had been ashamed of it at first. In the end he had decided that it was temperamental, inevitable, and had felt no further qualms. Emily had been healthy and beautiful when he married her. He had loved her then. But now—was it his fault that she was like this?

Mr Hutton dined alone. Food and drink left him more benevolent than he had been before dinner. To make amends for his show of exasperation he went up to his wife's room and offered to read to her. She was touched, gratefully accepted the offer, and Mr Hutton, who was particularly proud of his accent, suggested a little light reading in French.

'French? I am so fond of French.' Mrs Hutton spoke of the language of Racine as though it were a dish of green peas.

Mr Hutton ran down to the library and returned with a yellow volume. He began reading. The effort of pronouncing perfectly absorbed his whole attention. But how good his accent was! The fact of its goodness seemed to improve the quality of the novel he was reading.

At the end of fifteen pages an unmistakable sound aroused him. He looked up; Mrs Hutton had gone to sleep. He sat still for a little while, looking with a dispassionate curiosity at the sleeping face. Once it had been beautiful; once, long ago, the sight of it, the recollection of it, had moved him with an emotion profounder, perhaps, than any he had felt before or since. Now it was lined and cadaverous. The skin was stretched tightly over the cheekbones, across the bridge of the sharp, bird–like nose. The closed eyes were set in profound bone–rimmed sockets. The lamplight striking on the face from the side emphasised with light and shade its cavities and projections. It was the face of a dead Christ by Morales.

Le squelette était invisible
Au temps heureux de l'art païen.

He shivered a little, and tiptoed out of the room.

On the following day Mrs Hutton came down to luncheon. She had had some unpleasant palpitations during the night, but she was feeling better now. Besides, she wanted to do honour to her guest. Miss Spence listened to her complaints about Llandrindod Wells, and was loud in sympathy, lavish with advice. Whatever she said was always said with intensity. She leaned forward, aimed, so to speak, like a gun, and fired her words. Bang! the charge in her soul was ignited, the words whizzed forth at the narrow barrel of her mouth. She was a machine–gun riddling her hostess with sympathy. Mr Hutton had undergone similar bombardments, mostly of a literary or philosophic character—bombardments of Maeterlinck, of Mrs Besant, of Bergson, of William James. Today the missiles were medical. She talked about insomnia, she expatiated on the virtues of harmless drugs and beneficent specialists. Under the bombardment Mrs Hutton opened out, like a flower in the sun.

Mr Hutton looked on in silence. The spectacle of Janet Spence evoked in him an unfailing curiosity. He was not romantic enough to imagine that every face masked an interior physiognomy of beauty or strangeness, that every woman's small talk was like a vapour hanging over mysterious gulfs. His wife, for example, and Doris; they were nothing more than what they seemed to be. But with Janet Spence it was somehow different. Here one could be sure that there was some kind of a queer face behind the Gioconda smile and the Roman eyebrows. The only question was: What exactly was there? Mr Hutton could never quite make out.

'But perhaps you won't have to go to Llandrindod after all,' Miss Spence was saying. 'If you get well quickly Dr Libbard will let you off.'

'I only hope so. Indeed, I do really feel rather better today.'

Mr Hutton felt ashamed. How much was it his own lack of sympathy that prevented her from feeling well every day? But he comforted himself by reflecting that it was only a case of feeling, not of being better. Sympathy does not mend a diseased liver or a weak heart.

'My dear, I wouldn't eat those red currants if I were you,' he said, suddenly solicitous. 'You know that Libbard has banned everything with skins and pips.'

'But I am so fond of them,' Mrs Hutton protested, 'and I feel so well today.'

'Don't be a tyrant,' said Miss Spence, looking first at him and then at his wife. 'Let the poor invalid have what she fancies; it will do her good.' She laid her hand on Mrs Hutton's arm and patted it affectionately two or three times.

'Thank you, my dear.' Mrs Hutton helped herself to the stewed currants.

'Well, don't blame me if they make you ill again.'

'Do I ever blame you, dear?'

'You have nothing to blame me for,' Mr Hutton answered playfully. 'I am the perfect husband.'

They sat in the garden after luncheon. From the island of shade under the old cypress tree they looked out across a flat expanse of lawn, in which the parterres of flowers shone with a metallic brilliance.

Mr Hutton took a deep breath of the warm and fragrant air. 'It's good to be alive,' he said.

'Just to be alive,' his wife echoed, stretching one pale, knot–jointed hand into the sunlight.

A maid brought the coffee; the silver pots and

the little blue cups were set on a folding table near the group of chairs.

'Oh, my medicine!' exclaimed Mrs Hutton.

'Run in and fetch it, Clara, will you? The white bottle on the sideboard.'

'I'll go,' said Mr Hutton. 'I've got to go and fetch a cigar in any case.'

He ran in towards the house. On the threshold he turned round for an instant. The maid was walking back across the lawn. His wife was sitting up in her deck-chair, engaged in opening her white parasol. Miss Spence was bending over the table, pouring out the coffee. He passed into the cool obscurity of the house.

'Do you like sugar in your coffee?' Miss Spence inquired.

'Yes, please. Give me rather a lot. I'll drink it after my medicine to take the taste away.'

Mrs Hutton leaned back in her chair, lowering the sunshade over her eyes, so as to shut out from her vision the burning sky.

Behind her, Miss Spence was making a delicate clinking among the coffee–cups.

'I've given you three large spoonfuls. That ought to take the taste away. And here comes the medicine.'

Mr Hutton had reappeared, carrying a wineglass, half full of a pale liquid.

'It smells delicious,' he said, as he handed it to his wife.

'That's only the flavouring.' She drank it off at a gulp, shuddered, and made a grimace. 'Ugh, it's so nasty. Give me my coffee.'

Miss Spence gave her the cup; she sipped at it. 'You've made it like syrup. But it's very nice, after that atrocious medicine.'

At half–past three Mrs Hutton complained that she did not feel as well as she had done, and went indoors to lie down. Her husband would have said something about the red currants, but checked himself; the triumph of an 'I told you so' was too cheaply won. Instead, he was sympathetic, and gave her his arm to the house.

'A rest will do you good,' he said. 'By the way, I shan't be back till after dinner.'

'But why? Where are you going?'

'I promised to go to Johnson's this evening. We have to discuss the war memorial, you know.'

'Oh, I wish you weren't going.' Mrs Hutton was almost in tears. 'Can't you stay? I don't like being alone in the house.'

'But, my dear, I promised weeks ago.' It was a bother having to lie like this. 'And now I must get back and look after Miss Spence.'

He kissed her on the forehead and went out again into the garden. Miss Spence received him aimed and intense.

'Your wife is dreadfully ill,' she fired off at him.

'I thought she cheered up so much when you came.'

'That was purely nervous, purely nervous. I was watching her closely. With a heart in that condition and her digestion wrecked—yes, wrecked—anything might happen.'

'Libbard doesn't take so gloomy a view of poor Emily's health.' Mr Hutton held open the gate that led from the garden into the drive; Miss Spence's car was standing by the front door.

'Libbard is only a country doctor. You ought to see a specialist.'

He could not refrain from laughing. 'You have a macabre passion for specialists.'

Miss Spence held up her hand in protest. 'I am serious. I think poor Emily is in a very bad state. Anything might happen at any moment.'

He handed her into the car and shut the door. The chauffeur started the engine and climbed into his place, ready to drive off.

'Shall I tell him to start?' He had no desire to continue the conversation.

Miss Spence leaned forward and shot a Gioconda in his direction. 'Remember, I expect you to come and see me again soon.'

Mechanically he grinned, made a polite noise, and, as the car moved forward, waved his hand. He was happy to be alone.

A few minutes afterwards Mr Hutton himself drove away. Doris was waiting at the cross-roads. They dined together twenty miles from home, at a roadside hotel. It was one of those bad, expensive meals which are only cooked in country hotels frequented by motorists. It revolted Mr Hutton, but Doris enjoyed it. She always enjoyed things. Mr Hutton ordered a not very good brand of champagne. He was wishing he had spent the evening in his library.

When they started homewards Doris was a little tipsy and extremely affectionate. It was very dark inside the car, but looking forward, past the motionless form of M'Nab, they could see a bright and narrow universe of forms and colours scooped out of the night by the electric head–lamps.

It was after eleven when Mr Hutton reached home. Dr Libbard met him in the hall. He was a small man with delicate hands and well–formed features that were almost feminine. His brown eyes were large and melancholy. He used to waste a great deal of time sitting at the bedside of his patients, looking sadness through those eyes and talking in a sad, low voice about nothing in particular. His person exhaled a pleasing odour, decidedly antiseptic but at the same time suave and discreetly delicious.

'Libbard?' said Mr Hutton in surprise.

'You here? Is my wife ill?'

'We tried to fetch you earlier,' the soft, melancholy voice replied.

'It was thought you were at Mr Johnson's, but they

had no news of you there.'

'No, I was detained. I had a breakdown,' Mr Hutton answered irritably. It was tiresome to be caught out in a lie.

'Your wife wanted to see you urgently.'

'Well, I can go now.' Mr Hutton moved towards the stairs.

Dr Libbard laid a hand on his arm. 'I am afraid it's too late.'

'Too late?' He began fumbling with his watch; it wouldn't come out of the pocket.

'Mrs Hutton passed away half an hour ago.'

The voice remained even in its softness, the melancholy of the eyes did not deepen. Dr Libbard spoke of death as he would speak of a local cricket match. All things were equally vain and equally deplorable.

Mr Hutton found himself thinking of Janet Spence's words. At any moment—at any moment. She had been extraordinarily right.

'What happened?' he asked. 'What was the cause?'

Dr Libbard explained. It was heart failure brought on by a violent attack of nausea, caused in its turn by the eating of something of an irritant nature. Red currants? Mr Hutton suggested. Very likely. It had been too much for the heart. There was chronic valvular disease: something had collapsed under the strain. It was all over; she could not have suffered much.

III

'It's a pity they should have chosen the day of the Eton and Harrow match for the funeral,' old General Grego was saying as he stood, his top hat in his hand, under the shadow of the lych gate, wiping his face with his handkerchief.

Mr Hutton overheard the remark and with difficulty restrained a desire to inflict grievous bodily pain on the General. He would have liked to hit the old brute in the middle of his big red face. Monstrous great mulberry, spotted with meal! Was there no respect for the dead? Did nobody care? In theory he didn't much care; let the dead bury their dead. But here, at the graveside, he had found himself actually sobbing. Poor Emily, they had been pretty happy once. Now she was lying at the bottom of a seven-foot hole. And here was Grego complaining that he couldn't go to the Eton and Harrow match.

Mr Hutton looked round at the groups of black figures that were drifting slowly out of the churchyard towards the fleet of cabs and motors assembled in the road outside. Against the brilliant background of the July grass and flowers and foliage, they had a horribly alien and unnatural appearance. It pleased him to think that all these people would soon be dead, too.

That evening Mr Hutton sat up late in his library reading the life of Milton. There was no particular reason why he should have chosen Milton; it was the book that first came to hand, that was all. It was after midnight when he had finished. He got up from his armchair, unbolted the French windows, and stepped out on to the little paved terrace. The night was quiet and clear. Mr Hutton looked at the stars and at the holes between them, dropped his eyes to the dim lawns and hueless flowers of the garden, and let them wander over the farther landscape, black and grey under the moon.

He began to think with a kind of confused violence. There were the stars, there was Milton. A man can be somehow the peer of stars and night. Greatness, nobility. But is there seriously a difference between the noble and the ignoble? Milton, the stars, death, and himself—himself. The soul, the body; the higher and the lower nature. Perhaps there was something in it, after all. Milton had a god on his side and righteousness. What had he? Nothing, nothing whatever. There were only Doris's little breasts. What was the point of it all? Milton, the stars, death, and Emily in her grave, Doris and himself—always himself....

Oh, he was a futile and disgusting being. Everything convinced him of it. It was a solemn moment. He spoke aloud: 'I will, I will.' The sound of his own voice in the darkness was appalling; it seemed to him that he had sworn that infernal oath which binds even the gods: 'I will, I will.' There had been New Year's days and solemn anniversaries in the past, when he had felt the same contritions and recorded similar resolutions. They had all thinned away, these resolutions, like smoke, into nothingness. But this was a greater moment and he had pronounced a more fearful oath. In the future it was to be different. Yes, he would live by reason, he would be industrious, he would curb his appetites, he would devote his life to some good purpose. It was resolved and it would be so.

In practice he saw himself spending his mornings in agricultural pursuits, riding round with the bailiff, seeing that his land was farmed in the best modern way—silos and artificial manures and continuous cropping, and all that. The remainder of the day should be devoted to serious study. There was that book he had been intending to write for so long—The Effect of Diseases on Civilisation.

Mr Hutton went to bed humble and contrite, but with a sense that grace had entered into him. He slept for seven and a half hours, and woke to find the sun brilliantly shining. The emotions of the evening before had been transformed by a good night's rest into his customary cheerfulness. It was not until a good many seconds after his return to conscious life that he remembered his resolution, his Stygian oath. Milton and death seemed somehow different in the sunlight. As for the stars, they were not there. But the resolutions were good; even in the daytime he could see that. He had his horse saddled after breakfast, and rode round the farm with the bailiff. After luncheon he read Thucydides on the plague at Athens. In the evening he made a few notes on malaria in Southern Italy. While he was undressing he remembered that there was a good anecdote in Skelton's jest–book about the Sweating Sickness. He would have made a note of it if only he could have found a pencil.

On the sixth morning of his new life Mr Hutton found among his correspondence an envelope addressed in that peculiarly vulgar handwriting which he knew to be Doris's. He opened it, and began to read. She didn't know what to say; words were so inadequate. His wife dying like that, and so suddenly—it was too terrible. Mr Hutton sighed, but his interest revived somewhat as he read on:

'Death is so frightening, I never think of it when I can help it. But when something like this happens, or when I am feeling ill or depressed, then I can't help remembering it is there so close, and I think about all the wicked things I have done and about you and me, and I wonder what will happen, and I am so frightened. I am so lonely, Teddy Bear, and so unhappy, and I don't know what to do. I can't get rid of the idea of dying, I am so wretched and helpless without you. I didn't mean to write to you; I meant to wait till you were out of mourning and could come and see me again, but I was so lonely and miserable, Teddy Bear, I had to write. I couldn't help it. Forgive me, I want you so much; I have nobody in the world but you. You are so good and gentle and understanding; there is nobody like you. I shall never forget how good and kind you have been to me, and you are so clever and know so much, I can t understand how you ever came to pay any attention to me, I am so dull and stupid, much less like me and love me, because you do love me a little, don't you, Teddy Bear?'

Mr Hutton was touched with shame and remorse. To be thanked like this, worshipped for having seduced the girl—it was too much. It had just been a piece of imbecile wantonness. Imbecile, idiotic: there was no other way to describe it. For, when all was said, he had derived very little pleasure from it. Taking all things together, he had probably been more bored than amused. Once upon a time he had believed himself to be a hedonist. But to be a hedonist implies a certain process of reasoning, a deliberate choice of known pleasures, a rejection of known pains. This had been done without reason, against it. For he knew beforehand—so well, so well—that there was no interest or pleasure to be derived from these wretched affairs. And yet each time the vague itch came upon him he succumbed, involving himself once more in the old stupidity. There had been Maggie, his wife's maid, and Edith, the girl on the farm, and Mrs Pringle, and the waitress in London, and others—there seemed to be dozens of them. It had all been so stale and boring. He knew it would be; he always knew. And yet, and yet.... Experience doesn't teach.

Poor little Doris! He would write to her kindly, comfortingly, but he wouldn't see her again. A servant came to tell him that his horse was saddled and waiting. He mounted and rode off. That morning the old bailiff was more irritating than usual.

Five days later Doris and Mr Hutton ware sitting together on the pier at Southend; Doris, in white muslin with pink garnishings, radiated happiness; Mr Hutton, legs outstretched and chair tilted, had pushed the panama back from his forehead, and was trying to feel like a tripper. That night, when Doris was asleep, breathing and warm by his side, he recaptured, in this moment of darkness and physical fatigue, the rather cosmic emotion which had possessed him that evening, not a fortnight ago, when he had made his great resolution. And so his solemn oath had already gone the way of so many other resolutions. Unreason had triumphed; at the first itch of desire he had given way. He was hopeless, hopeless.

For a long time he lay with closed eyes, ruminating his humiliation. The girl stirred in her sleep, Mr Hutton turned over and looked in her direction. Enough faint light crept in between the half-drawn curtains to show her bare arm and shoulder, her neck, and the dark tangle of hair on the pillow. She was beautiful, desirable. Why did he lie there moaning over his sins? What did it matter? If he were hopeless, then so be it; he would make the best of his hopelessness. A glorious sense of irresponsibility suddenly filled him. He was free, magnificently free. In a kind of exaltation he drew the girl towards him. She woke, bewildered, almost frightened under his rough kisses.

The storm of his desire subsided into a kind of serene merriment. The whole atmosphere seemed to be quivering with enormous silent laughter.

'Could anyone love you as much as I do, Teddy Bear?' The question came faintly from distant worlds of love.

'I think I know somebody who does,' Mr Hutton replied. The submarine laughter was swelling, rising, ready to break the surface of silence and resound.

'Who? Tell me. What do you mean?' The voice had come very close; charged with suspicion, anguish, indignation, it belonged to this immediate world.

'A—ah!'

'Who?'

'You'll never guess.' Mr Hutton kept up the joke until it began to grow tedious, and then pronounced the name 'Janet Spence.'

Doris was incredulous. 'Miss Spence of the Manor? That old woman?' It was too ridiculous. Mr Hutton laughed too.

'But it's quite true,' he said. 'She adores me.' Oh, the vast joke. He would go and see her as soon as he returned—see and conquer. 'I believe she wants to marry me,' he added.

'But you wouldn't ... you don't intend....'

The air was fairly crepitating with humour. Mr Hutton laughed aloud. 'I intend to marry you,' he said. It seemed to him the best joke he had ever made in his life.

When Mr Hutton left Southend he was once more a married man. It was agreed that, for the time being, the fact should be kept secret. In the autumn they would go abroad together, and the world should be informed. Meanwhile he was to go back to his own house and Doris to hers.

The day after his return he walked over in the afternoon to see Miss Spence. She received him with the old Gioconda.

'I was expecting you to come.'

'I couldn't keep away,' Mr Hutton gallantly replied.

They sat in the summer-house. It was a pleasant place—a little old stucco temple bowered among dense bushes of evergreen. Miss Spence had left her mark on it by hanging up over the seat a blue–and–white Della Robbia plaque.

'I am thinking of going to Italy this autumn,' said Mr Hutton. He felt like a ginger–beer bottle, ready to pop with bubbling humorous excitement.

'Italy....' Miss Spence closed her eyes ecstatically. 'I feel drawn there too.'

'Why not let yourself be drawn?'

'I don't know. One somehow hasn't the energy and initiative to set out alone.'

'Alone....' Ah, sound of guitars and throaty singing. 'Yes, travelling alone isn't much fun.'

Miss Spence lay back in her chair without speaking. Her eyes were still closed. Mr Hutton stroked his moustache. The silence prolonged itself for what seemed a very long time.

Pressed to stay to dinner, Mr Hutton did not refuse.

The fun had hardly started. The table was laid in the loggia. Through its arches they looked out on to the sloping garden, to the valley below and the farther hills. Light ebbed away; the heat and silence were oppressive. A huge cloud was mounting up the sky, and there were distant breathings of thunder. The thunder drew nearer, a wind began to blow, and the first drops of rain fell. The table was cleared. Miss Spence and Mr Hutton sat on in the growing darkness.

Miss Spence broke a long silence by saying meditatively.

'I think everyone has a right to a certain amount of happiness, don't you?'

'Most certainly.' But what was she leading up to? Nobody makes generalisations about life unless they mean to talk about themselves. Happiness: he looked back on his own life, and saw a cheerful, placid existence disturbed by no great griefs or discomforts or alarms. He had always had money and freedom; he had been able to do very much as he wanted. Yes, he supposed he had been happy—happier than most men. And now he was not merely happy; he had discovered in irresponsibility the secret of gaiety. He was about to say something about his happiness when Miss Spence went on speaking.

'People like you and me have a right to be happy some time in our lives.'

'Me?' said Mr Hutton surprised.

'Poor Henry! Fate hasn't treated either of us very well.'

'Oh, well, it might have treated me worse.'

'You re being cheerful. That's brave of you. But don't think I can't see behind the mask.'

Miss Spence spoke louder and louder as the rain came down more and more heavily. Periodically the thunder cut across her utterances. She talked on, shouting against the noise.

'I have understood you so well and for so long.'

A flash revealed her, aimed and intent, leaning towards him. Her eyes were two profound and menacing gun–barrels. The darkness re–engulfed her.

'You were a lonely soul seeking a companion soul. I could sympathise with you in your solitude. Your marriage ...'

The thunder cut short the sentence. Miss Spence's voice became audible once more with the words:

'... could offer no companionship to a man of your stamp. You needed a soul mate.'

A soul mate—he! a soul mate. It was incredibly fantastic. Georgette Leblanc, the ex–soul mate of Maurice Maeterlinck. He had seen that in the paper a few days ago. So it was thus that Janet Spence had painted him in her imagination—a soul–mater. And for Doris he was a picture of goodness and the cleverest man in the world. And actually, really, he was what?—Who knows?

'My heart went out to you. I could understand; I was lonely, too.' Miss Spence laid her hand on his knee. 'You were so patient.' Another flash. She was still aimed, dangerously. 'You never complained. But I could guess—I could guess.'

'How wonderful of you!' So he was an âme incomprise.

'Only a woman's intuition....'

The thunder crashed and rumbled, died away, and only the sound of the rain was left. The thunder was his laughter, magnified, externalised. Flash and crash, there it was again, right on top of them.

'Don't you feel that you have within you something that is akin to this storm?' He could imagine her leaning forward as she uttered the words. 'Passion makes one the equal of the elements.'

What was his gambit now? Why, obviously, he should have said 'Yes,' and ventured on some unequivocal gesture. But Mr Hutton suddenly took fright. The ginger beer in him had gone flat. The woman was serious—terribly serious. He was appalled.

Passion? 'No,' he desperately answered. 'I am without passion.'

But his remark was either unheard or unheeded, for Miss Spence went on with a growing exaltation, speaking so rapidly, however, and in such a burningly intimate whisper that Mr Hutton found it very difficult to distinguish what she was saying. She was telling him, as far as he could make out, the story of her life. The lightning was less frequent now, and there were long intervals of darkness.

But at each flash he saw her still aiming towards him, still yearning forward with a terrifying intensity. Darkness, the rain, and then flash! her face was there, close at hand. A pale mask, greenish white; the large eyes, the narrow barrel of the mouth, the heavy eyebrows. Agrippina, or wasn't it rather—yes, wasn't it rather George Robey?

He began devising absurd plans for escaping. He might suddenly jump up, Pretending he had seen a burglar—Stop thief, stop thief!—and dash off into the night in pursuit. Or should he say that he felt faint, a heart attack? or that he had seen, a ghost—Emily's ghost—in the garden? Absorbed in his childish plotting, he had ceased to pay any attention to Miss Spence's words. The spasmodic clutching of her hand recalled his thoughts.

'I honoured you for that, Henry,' she was saying.

Honoured him for what?

'Marriage is a sacred tie, and your respect for it, even when the marriage was, as it was in your case, an unhappy one, made me respect you and admire you, and—shall I dare say the word?—'

Oh, the burglar, the ghost in the garden! But it was too late.

'... yes, love you, Henry, all the more. But we're free now, Henry.'

Free? There was a movement in the dark, and she was kneeling on the floor by his chair.

'Oh, Henry, Henry, I have been unhappy too.'

Her arms embraced him, and by the shaking of her body he could feel that she was sobbing. She might have been a suppliant crying for mercy.

'You mustn't, Janet,' he protested. Those tears were terrible, terrible. 'Not now, not now! You must be calm; you must go to bed.' He patted her shoulder, then got up, disengaging himself from her embrace. He left her still crouching on the floor beside the chair on which he had been sitting.

Groping his way into the hall, and without waiting to look for his hat, he went out of the house, taking infinite pains to close the front door noiselessly behind him. The clouds had blown over, and the moon was shining from a clear sky. There were puddles all along the road, and a noise of running water rose from the gutters and ditches. Mr Hutton splashed along, not caring if he got wet.

How heartrendingly she had sobbed! With the emotions of pity and remorse that the recollection evoked in him there was a certain resentment: why couldn't she have played the game that he was playing the heartless, amusing game? Yes, but he had known all the time that she wouldn't, she couldn't play that game; he had known and persisted.

What had she said about passion and the elements? Something absurdly stale, but true, true. There she was, a cloud black bosomed and charged with thunder, and he, like some absurd little Benjamin Franklin, had sent up a kite into the heart of the menace. Now he was complaining that his toy had drawn the lightning.

She was probably still kneeling by that chair in the loggia, crying.

But why hadn't he been able to keep up the game? Why had his irresponsibility deserted him, leaving him suddenly sober in a cold world? There were no answers to any of his questions. One idea burned steady and luminous in his mind—the idea of flight. He must get away at once.

IV

'What are you thinking about, Teddy Bear?'

'Nothing.'

There was a silence. Mr Hutton remained motionless, his elbows on the parapet of the terrace, his chin in his hands, looking down over Florence. He had taken a villa on one of the hilltops to the south of the city. From a little raised terrace at the end of the garden one looked down a long fertile valley on to the town and beyond it to the bleak mass of Monte Morello and, eastward of it, to the peopled hill of Fiesole, dotted with white houses. Everything was clear and luminous in the September sunshine.

'Are you worried about anything?'

'No, thank you.'

'Tell me, Teddy Bear.'

'But, my dear, there's nothing to tell.' Mr Hutton

turned round, smiled, and patted the girl's hand. 'I think you'd better go in and have your siesta. It's too hot for you here.'

'Very well, Teddy Bear. Are you coming too?'

'When I've finished my cigar.'

'All right. But do hurry up and finish it, Teddy Bear.' Slowly, reluctantly, she descended the steps of the terrace and walked towards the house.

Mr Hutton continued his contemplation of Florence. He had need to be alone. It was good sometimes to escape from Doris and the restless solicitude of her passion. He had never known the pains of loving hopelessly, but he was experiencing now the pains of being loved. These last weeks had been a period of growing discomfort. Doris was always with him, like an obsession, like a guilty conscience. Yes, it was good to be alone.

He pulled an envelope out of his pocket and opened it; not without reluctance. He hated letters; they always contained something unpleasant—nowadays, since his second marriage. This was from his sister. He began skimming through the insulting home–truths of which it was composed. The words 'indecent haste,' 'social suicide,' 'scarcely cold in her grave,' 'person of the lower classes,' all occurred. They were inevitable now in any communication from a well–meaning and right–thinking relative. Impatient, he was about to tear the stupid letter to pieces when his eye fell on a sentence at the bottom of the third page. His heart beat with uncomfortable violence as he read it. It was too monstrous! Janet Spence was going about telling everyone that he had poisoned his wife in order to marry Doris. What damnable malice! Ordinarily a man of the suavest temper, Mr Hutton found himself trembling with rage. He took the childish satisfaction of calling names—he cursed the woman.

Then suddenly he saw the ridiculous side of the situation. The notion that he should have murdered anyone in order to marry Doris! If they only knew how miserably bored he was. Poor, dear Janet! She had tried to be malicious; she had only succeeded in being stupid.

A sound of footsteps aroused him; he looked round. In the garden below the little terrace the servant girl of the house was picking fruit. A Neapolitan, strayed somehow as far north as Florence, she was a specimen of the classical type—a little debased. Her profile might have been taken from a Sicilian coin of a bad period. Her features, carved floridly in the grand tradition, expressed an almost perfect stupidity. Her mouth was the most beautiful thing about her; the calligraphic hand of nature had richly curved it into an expression of mulish bad temper.... Under her hideous black clothes, Mr Hutton divined a powerful body, firm and massive. He had looked at her before with a vague interest and curiosity. Today the curiosity defined and focused itself into a desire. An idyll of Theocritus. Here was the woman; he, alas, was not precisely like a goatherd on the volcanic hills. He called to her.

'Armida!'

The smile with which she answered him was so provocative, attested so easy a virtue, that Mr Hutton took fright. He was on the brink once more—on the brink. He must draw back, oh! quickly, quickly, before it was too late. The girl continued to look up at him.

'Ha chiamito?' she asked at last.

Stupidity or reason? Oh, there was no choice now. It was imbecility every time.

'Scendo' he called back to her. Twelve steps led from the garden to the terrace. Mr Hutton counted them. Down, down, down, down.... He saw a vision of himself descending from one circle of the inferno to the next—from a darkness full of wind and hail to an abyss of stinking mud.

V

For a good many days the Hutton case had a place on the front page of every newspaper. There had been no more popular murder trial since George Smith had temporarily eclipsed the European War by drowning in a warm bath his seventh bride. The public imagination was stirred by this tale of a murder brought to light months after the date of the crime. Here, it was felt, was one of those incidents in human life, so notable because they are so rare, which do definitely justify the ways of God to man. A wicked man had been moved by an illicit passion to kill his wife. For months he had lived in sin and fancied security——only to be dashed at last more horribly into the pit he had prepared for himself. Murder will out, and here was a case of it. The readers of the newspapers were in a position to follow every movement of the hand of God. There had been vague, but persistent, rumours in the neighbourhood; the police had taken action at last. Then came the exhumation order, the post–mortem examination, the inquest, the evidence of the experts, the verdict of the coroner's jury, the trial, the condemnation. For once Providence had done its duty, obviously, grossly, didactically, as in a melodrama. The newspapers were right in making of the case the staple intellectual food of a whole season.

Mr Hutton's first emotion when he was summoned from Italy to give evidence at the inquest was one of indignation. It was a monstrous, a scandalous thing that the police should take such idle, malicious gossip seriously. When the inquest was over he would bring an action for malicious prosecution against the Chief Constable; he would sue the Spence woman for slander.

The inquest was opened; the astonishing evidence unrolled itself. The experts had examined the body, and had found traces of arsenic; they were of opinion that the late Mrs Hutton had died of arsenic poisoning.

Arsenic poisoning.... Emily had died of arsenic poisoning? After that, Mr Hutton learned with surprise that there was enough arsenicated insecticide in his green–houses to poison an army.

It was now, quite suddenly, that he saw it: there was a case against him. Fascinated, he watched it growing, growing, like some monstrous tropical plant. It was enveloping him, surrounding him; he was lost in a tangled forest.

When was the poison administered? The experts agreed that it must have been swallowed eight or nine hours before death. About lunch–time? Yes, about lunch–time. Clara, the parlour–maid, was called. Mrs Hutton, she remembered, had asked her to go and fetch her medicine. Mr Hutton had volunteered to go instead; he had gone alone. Miss Spence—ah, the memory of the storm, the white aimed face! the horror of it all!—Miss Spence confirmed Clara's statement, and added that Mr Hutton had come back with the medicine already poured out in a wineglass, not in the bottle.

Mr Hutton's indignation evaporated. He was dismayed, frightened. It was all too fantastic to be taken seriously, and yet this nightmare was a fact it was actually happening.

M'Nab had seen them kissing, often. He had taken them for a drive on the day of Mrs Hutton's death. He could see them reflected in the wind–screen, sometimes out of the tail of his eye.

The inquest was adjourned. That evening Doris went to bed with a headache. When he went to her room after dinner, Mr Hutton found her crying.

'What's the matter?' He sat down on the edge of her bed and began to stroke her hair. For a long time she did not answer, and he went on stroking her hair mechanically, almost unconsciously; sometimes, even he bent down and kissed her bare shoulder. He had his own affairs, however, to think about. What had happened? How was it that the stupid gossip had actually come true? Emily had died of arsenic poisoning. It was absurd, impossible. The order of things had been broken, and he was at the mercy of an irresponsibility. What had happened, what was going to happen? He was interrupted in the midst of his thoughts.

'It's my fault—it's my fault!' Doris suddenly sobbed out. 'I shouldn't have loved you; I oughtn't to have let you love me. Why was I ever born?'

Mr Hutton didn't say anything but looked down in silence at the abject figure of misery lying on the bed.

'If they do anything to you I shall kill myself.'

She sat up, held him for a moment at arm's length, and looked at him with a kind of violence, as though she were never to see him again.

'I love you, I love you, I love you.' She drew him, inert and passive, towards her, clasped him, pressed herself against him. 'I didn't know you loved me as much as that, Teddy Bear. But why did you do it—why did you do it?'

Mr Hutton undid her clasping arms and got up. His face became very red. 'You seem to take it for granted that I murdered my wife,' he said. 'It's really too grotesque.

What do you all take me for? A cinema hero?' He had begun to lose his temper. All the exasperation, all the fear and bewilderment of the day, was transformed into a violent anger against her. 'It's all such damned stupidity. Haven't you any conception of a civilised man's mentality? Do I look the sort of man who'd go about slaughtering people? I suppose you imagined I was so insanely in love with you that I could commit any folly. When will you women understand that one isn't insanely in love? All one asks for is a quiet life, which you won't allow one to have. I don't know what the devil ever induced me to marry you. It was all a damned stupid, practical joke. And now you go about saying I'm a murderer. I won't stand it.'

Mr Hutton stamped towards the door. He had said horrible things, he knew—odious things that he ought speedily to unsay. But he wouldn't. He closed the door behind him.

'Teddy Bear!' He turned the handle; the latch clicked into place. Teddy Bear! The voice that came to him through the closed door was agonised. Should he go back? He ought to go back. He touched the handle, then withdrew his fingers and quickly walked away. When he was half-way down the stairs he halted. She might try to do something silly—throw herself out of the window or God knows what! He listened attentively; there was no sound. But he pictured her very clearly, tiptoeing across the room, lifting the sash as high as it would go, leaning out into the cold night air. It was raining a little. Under the window lay the paved terrace. How far below? Twenty–five or thirty feet? Once, when he was walking along Piccadilly, a dog had jumped out of a third–storey window of the Ritz. He had seen it fall; he had heard it strike the pavement. Should he go back? He was damned if he would; he hated her.

He sat for a long time in the library. What had happened? What was happening? He turned the question over and over in his mind and could find no answer. Suppose the nightmare dreamed itself out to its horrible conclusion. Death was waiting for him. His eyes filled with tears; he wanted so passionately to live. 'Just to be alive.' Poor Emily had wished it too, he remembered: 'Just to be alive.' There were still so many places in this astonishing world unvisited, so many queer delightful people still unknown, so many lovely women never so much as seen. The huge white oxen would still be dragging their wains along the Tuscan roads, the cypresses would still go up, straight as pillars, to the blue heaven; but he would not be there to see them. And the sweet southern wines—Tear of Christ and Blood of Judas—others would drink them, not he. Others would walk down the obscure and narrow lanes between the bookshelves in the London Library, sniffing the dusty perfume of good literature, peering at strange titles, discovering unknown names, exploring the fringes of vast domains of knowledge. He would be lying in a hole in the ground. And why, why? Confusedly he felt that some extraordinary kind of justice was being done. In the past he had been wanton and imbecile and irresponsible. Now Fate was playing as wantonly, as irresponsibly, with him. It was tit for tat, and God existed after all.

He felt that he would like to pray. Forty years ago he used to kneel by his bed every evening. The nightly formula of his childhood came to him almost unsought from some long unopened chamber of the memory. 'God bless Father and Mother, Tom and Cissie and the Baby, Mademoiselle and Nurse, and everyone that I love, and make me a good boy. Amen.' They were all dead now all except Cissie.

His mind seemed to soften and dissolve; a great calm descended upon his spirit. He went upstairs to ask Doris's forgiveness. He found her lying on the couch at the foot of the bed. On the floor beside her stood a blue bottle of liniment, marked 'Not to be taken'; she seemed to have drunk about half of it.

'You didn't love me,' was all she said when she opened her eyes to find him bending over her.

Dr Libbard arrived in time to prevent any very serious consequences. 'You mustn't do this again,' he said while Mr Hutton was out of the room.

'What's to prevent me?' she asked defiantly.

Dr Libbard looked at her with his large, sad eyes. 'There's nothing to prevent you,' he said. 'Only yourself and your baby. Isn't it rather bad luck on your baby, not allowing it to come into the world because you want to go out of it?'

Doris was silent for a time. 'All right,' she whispered. 'I won't.'

Mr Hutton sat by her bedside for the rest of the night. He felt himself now to be indeed a murderer. For a time he persuaded himself that he loved this pitiable child. Dozing in his chair, he woke up, stiff and cold, to find himself drained dry, as it were, of every emotion. He had become nothing but a tired and suffering carcase. At six o'clock he undressed and went to bed for a couple of hours' sleep. In the course of the same afternoon the coroner's jury brought in a verdict of 'Wilful Murder,' and Mr Hutton was committed for trial.

VI

Miss Spence was not at all well. She had found her public appearances in the witness–box very trying, and when it was all over she had something that was very nearly a breakdown. She slept badly, and suffered from nervous indigestion. Dr Libbard used to call every other day. She talked to him a great deal—mostly about the Hutton case.... Her moral indignation was always on the boil. Wasn't it appalling to think that one had had a murderer in one's house. Wasn't it extraordinary that one could have been for so long mistaken about the man's character? (But she had had an inkling from the first.) And then the girl he had gone off with—so low class, so little better than a prostitute. The news that the second Mrs Hutton was expecting a baby the posthumous child of a condemned and executed criminal—revolted her; the thing was shocking an obscenity. Dr Libbard answered her gently and vaguely, and prescribed bromide.

One morning he interrupted her in the midst of her customary tirade. 'By the way,' he said in his soft, melancholy voice, 'I suppose it was really you who poisoned Mrs Hutton.'

Miss Spence stared at him for two or three seconds with enormous eyes, and then quietly said, 'Yes.' After that she started to cry.

'In the coffee, I suppose.'

She seemed to nod assent. Dr Libbard took out his fountain–pen, and in his neat, meticulous calligraphy wrote out a prescription for a sleeping draught.

H F Arnold

(1902-1963)

An American science fiction writer active in the 1930s. Though he published only a handful of stories, his work *The Night Wire* is considered a classic weird tale. Surprisingly little is known about his life.

The Night Wire
H F Arnold

'New York, September 30 CP FLASH

'Ambassador Holliwell died here today. The end came suddenly as the ambassador was alone in his study....'

There's something ungodly about these night wire jobs. You sit up here on the top floor of a skyscraper and listen in to the whispers of a civilization. New York, London, Calcutta, Bombay, Singapore—they're your next–door neighbors after the street lights go dim and the world has gone to sleep.

Along in the quiet hours between 2 and 4, the receiving operators doze over their sounders and the news comes in. Fires and disasters and suicides. Murders, crowds, catastrophes. Sometimes an earthquake with a casualty list as long as your arm. The night wire man takes it down almost in his sleep, picking it off on his typewriter with one finger.

Once in a long time you prick up your ears and listen.

You've heard of someone you knew in Singapore, Halifax or Paris, long ago. Maybe they've been promoted, but more probably they've been murdered or drowned. Perhaps they just decided to quit and took some bizarre way out. Made it interesting enough to get in the news.

But that doesn't happen often. Most of the time you sit and doze and tap, tap on your typewriter and wish you were home in bed.

Sometimes, though, queer things happen. One did the other night and I haven't got over it yet. I wish I could.

You see, I handle the night manager's desk in a western seaport town; what the name is, doesn't matter.

There is, or rather was, only one night operator on my staff, a fellow named John Morgan, about forty years of age, I should say, and a sober, hard–working sort.

He was one of the best operators I ever knew, what is known as a 'double' man. That means he could handle two instruments at once and type the stories on different typewriters at the same time. He was one of the three men I ever knew who could do it consistently, hour after hour, and never make a mistake.

Generally we used only one wire at night, but sometimes, when it was late and the news was coming fast, the Chicago and Denver stations would open a second wire and then Morgan would do his stuff. He was a wizard, a mechanical automatic wizard which functioned marvelously but was without imagination.

On the night of the sixteenth he complained of feeling tired. It was the first and last time I had ever heard him say a word about himself, and I had known him for three years.

It was at just 3 o'clock and we were running only one wire. I was nodding over reports at my desk and not paying much attention to him when he spoke.

'Jim,' he said, 'does it feel close in here to you?'

'Why, no, John,' I answered, 'but I'll open a window if you like.'

'Never mind,' he said. 'I reckon I'm just a little tired.'

That was all that was said and I went on working. Every ten minutes or so I would walk over and take a pile of copy that had stacked up neatly beside his typewriter as the messages were printed out in triplicate.

It must have been twenty minutes after he spoke that I noticed he had opened up the other wire and was using both typewriters. I thought it was a little unusual, as there was nothing very 'hot' coming in. On my next trip I picked up the copy from both machines and took it back to my desk to sort out the duplicates.

The first wire was running out the usual sort of stuff and I just looked over it hurriedly. Then I turned to the second pile of copy. I remember it particularly because the story was from a town I had never heard of: 'Xebico.' Here is the dispatch. I saved a duplicate of it from our files:

'Xebico Sept. 16 CP BULLETIN

'The heaviest mist in the history of the city settled over

the town at 4 o'clock yesterday afternoon. All traffic has stopped and the mist hangs like a pall over everything. Lights of ordinary intensity fail to pierce the fog, which is constantly growing heavier.

'Scientists here are unable to agree as to the cause, and the local weather bureau states that the like has never occurred before in the history of the city.

'At 7 p. m. last night municipal authorities—(more)'

That was all there was. Nothing out of the ordinary at a bureau headquarters, but, as I say, I noticed the story because of the name of the town.

It must have been fifteen minutes later that I went over for another batch of copy. Morgan was slumped down in his chair and had switched his green electric light shade so that the gleam missed his eyes and hit only the top of the two typewriters.

Only the usual stuff was in the right hand pile, but the left hand batch carried another story from 'Xebico.' All press dispatches come in 'takes,' meaning that parts of many different stories are strung along together, perhaps with but a few paragraphs of each coming through at a time. This second story was marked 'add fog.' Here is the copy:

'At 7 p. m. the fog had increased noticeably. All lights were now invisible and the town was shrouded in pitch darkness.

'As a peculiarity of the phenomenon, the fog is accompanied by a sickly odor, comparable to nothing yet experienced here.'

Below that in customary press fashion was the hour, 3:27, and the initials of the operator, JM.

There was only one other story in the pile from the second wire. Here it is:

'2nd add Xebico Fog

'Accounts as to the origin of the mist differ greatly. Among the most unusual is that of the sexton of the local church, who groped his way to headquarters in a hysterical condition and declared that the fog originated in the village churchyard.

"It was first visible in the shape of a soft gray blanket clinging to the earth above the graves,' he stated. 'Then it began to rise, higher and higher. A subterranean breeze seemed to blow it in billows, which split up and then joined together again.

"Fog phantoms, writhing in anguish, twisted the mist into queer forms and figures. And then—in the very thick midst of the mass—something moved.

"I turned and ran from the accursed spot. Behind me I heard screams coming from the houses bordering on the graveyard.'

'Although the sexton's story is generally discredited, a party has left to investigate. Immediately after telling his story, the sexton collapsed and is now in a local hospital, unconscious.'

Queer story, wasn't it? Not that we aren't used to it, for

a lot of unusual stories come in over the wire. But for some reason or other, perhaps because it was so quiet that night, the report of the fog made a great impression on me.

It was almost with dread that I went over to the waiting piles of copy. Morgan did not move and the only sound in the room was the tap–tap of the sounders. It was ominous, nerve–racking.

There was another story from Xebico in the pile of copy. I seized on it anxiously.

'New Lead Xebico Fog CP

'The rescue party which went out at 11 p. m. to investigate a weird story of the origin of a fog which, since late yesterday, has shrouded the city in darkness, has failed to return. Another and larger party has been dispatched.

'Meanwhile the fog has, if possible, grown heavier. It seeps through the cracks in the doors and fills the atmosphere with a terribly depressing odor of decay. It is oppressive, terrifying, bearing with it a subtle impression of things long dead.

'Residents of the city have left their homes and gathered in the local church, where the priests are holding services of prayer. The scene is beyond description. Grown folk and children are alike terrified and many are almost beside themselves with fear.

'Mid the wisps of vapor which partially veil the church auditorium, an old priest is praying for the welfare of his flock. The audience alternately wail and cross themselves.

'From the outskirts of the city may be heard cries of unknown voices. They echo through the fog in queer uncadenced minor keys. The sounds resemble nothing so much as wind whistling through a gigantic tunnel. But the night is calm and there is no wind. The second rescue party—(more)'

I am a calm man and never in a dozen years spent with the wires have been known to become excited, but despite myself I rose from my chair and walked to the window.

Could I be mistaken, or far down in the canyons of the city beneath me did I see a faint trace of fog? Pshaw! It was all imagination.

In the pressroom the click of the sounders seemed to have raised the tempo of their tune. Morgan alone had not stirred from his chair. His head sunk between his shoulders, he tapped the dispatches out on the typewriters with one finger of each hand.

He looked asleep. Maybe he was—but no, endlessly, efficiently, the two machines rattled off line after line, as relentless and effortless as death itself. There was something about the monotonous movement of the typewriter keys that fascinated me. I walked over and stood behind his chair reading over his shoulder the type as it came into being, word by word.

Ah, here was another:

'Flash Xebico CP

'There will be no more bulletins from this office. The

impossible has happened. No messages have come into this room for twenty minutes. We are cut off from the outside and even the streets below us.

'I will stay with the wire until the end.

'It is the end, indeed. Since 4 p. m. yesterday the fog has hung over the city. Following reports from the sexton of the local church, two rescue parties were sent out to investigate conditions on the outskirts of the city. Neither party has ever returned nor was any word received from them. It is quite certain now that they will never return.

'From my instrument I can gaze down on the city beneath me. From the position of this room on the thirteenth floor, nearly the entire city can be seen. Now I can see only a thick blanket of blackness where customarily are lights and life.

'I fear greatly that the wailing cries heard constantly from the outskirts of the city are the death cries of the inhabitants. They are constantly increasing in volume and are approaching the center of the city.

'The fog yet hangs over everything. If possible, it is even heavier than before. But the conditions have changed. Instead of an opaque, impenetrable wall of odorous vapor, now swirls and writhes a shapeless mass in contortions of almost human agony. Now and again the mass parts and I catch a brief glimpse of the streets below.

'People are running to and fro, screaming in despair. A vast bedlam of sound flies up to my window, and above all is the immense whistling of unseen and unfelt winds.

'The fog has again swept over the city and the whistling is coming closer and closer.

'It is now directly beneath me.

'God! An instant ago the mist opened and I caught a glimpse of the streets below.

'The fog is not simply vapor—it lives. By the side of each moaning and weeping human is a companion figure, an aura of strange and varicolored hues. How the shapes cling! Each to a living thing!

'The men and women are down. Flat on their faces. The fog figures caress them lovingly. They are kneeling beside them. They are—but I dare not tell it.

'The prone and writhing bodies have been stripped of their clothing. They are being consumed—piecemeal.

'A merciful wall of hot, steamy vapor has swept over the whole scene. I can see no more.

'Beneath me the wall of vapor is changing colors. It seems to be lighted by internal fires. No, it isn't. I have made a mistake. The colors are from above, reflections from the sky.

'Look up! Look up! The whole sky is in flames. Colors as yet unseen by man or demon. The flames are moving, they have started to intermix, the colors rearrange themselves. They are so brilliant that my eyes burn, yet they are a long way off.

'Now they have begun to swirl, to circle in and

out, twisting in intricate designs and patterns. The lights are racing each with each, a kaleidoscope of unearthly brilliance.

'I have made a discovery. There is nothing harmful in the lights. They radiate force and friendliness, almost cheeriness. But by their very strength, they hurt.

'As I look they are swinging closer and closer, a million miles at each jump. Millions of miles with the speed of light. Aye, it is light, the quintessence of all light. Beneath it the fog melts into a jeweled mist, radiant, rainbow–colored of a thousand varied spectrums.

'I can see the streets. Why, they are filled with people! The lights are coming closer. They are all around me. I am enveloped. I——'

The message stopped abruptly. The wire to Xebico was dead. Beneath my eyes in the narrow circle of light from under the green lampshade, the black printing no longer spun itself, letter by letter, across the page.

The room seemed filled with a solemn quiet, a silence vaguely impressive. Powerful.

I looked down at Morgan. His hands had dropped nervelessly at his sides while his body had hunched over peculiarly. I turned the lampshade back, throwing the light squarely in his face. His eyes were staring, fixed. Filled with a sudden foreboding, I stepped beside him and called Chicago on the wire. After a second the sounder clicked its answer.

Why? But there was something wrong. Chicago was reporting that Wire Two had not been used throughout the evening.

'Morgan!' I shouted. 'Morgan! Wake up, it isn't true. Someone has been hoaxing us. Why——' In my eagerness I grasped him by the shoulder. It was only then that I understood.

The body was quite cold. Morgan had been dead for hours. Could it be that his sensitized brain and automatic fingers had continued to record impressions even after the end?

I shall never know, for I shall never again handle the night shift. Search in a world atlas discloses no town of Xebico. Whatever it was that killed John Morgan will forever remain a mystery.

William Hope Hodgson

(1877-1918)

Wrote atmospheric horror and fantasy stories, including *The House on the Borderland* and *The Night Land.* He worked as a sailor, which influenced his maritime horror stories. He died in World War I while serving as an artillery officer.

The Derelict

William Hope Hodgson

'It's the material,' said the old ship's doctor—'the material plus the conditions—and, maybe,' he added slowly, 'a third factor—yes, a third factor; but there, there—' He broke off his half-meditative sentence and began to charge his pipe.

'Go on, doctor,' we said encouragingly, and with more than a little expectancy. We were in the

smoke-room of the Sand-a-lea, running across the North Atlantic; and the doctor was a character. He concluded the charging of his pipe, and lit it; then settled himself, and began to express himself more fully.

'The material,' he said with conviction, 'is inevitably the medium of expression of the life–force—the fulcrum, as it were; lacking which it is unable to exert itself, or, indeed, to express itself in any form or fashion that would be intelligible or evident to us. So potent is the share of the material in the production of that thing which we name life, and so eager the life–force to express itself, that I am convinced it would, if given the right conditions, make itself manifest even through so hopeless seeming a medium as a simple block of sawn wood; for I tell you, gentlemen, the life–force is both as fiercely urgent and as indiscriminate as fire—the destructor; yet which some are now growing to consider the very essence of life rampant. There is a quaint seeming paradox there,' he concluded, nodding his old grey head.

'Yes, doctor,' I said. 'In brief, your argument is that life is a thing, state, fact, or element, call it what you like, which requires the material through which to manifest itself, and that given the material, plus the conditions, the result is life. In other words, that life is an evolved product, manifested through matter and bred of conditions—eh?'

'As we understand the word,' said the old doctor.

'Though, mind you, there may be a third factor. But, in my heart, I believe that it is a matter of chemistry—conditions and a suitable medium; but given the conditions, the brute is so almighty that it will seize upon anything through which to manifest itself. It is a force generated by conditions; but, nevertheless, this does not bring us one iota nearer to its explanation, any more than to the explanation of electricity or fire. They are, all three, of the outer forces—monsters of the void. Nothing we can do will create any one of them, our power is merely to be able, by providing the conditions, to make each one of them manifest to our physical senses. Am I clear?'

'Yes, doctor, in a way, you are,' I said. 'But I don't agree with you, though I think I understand you.

Electricity and fire are both what I might call natural things, but life is an abstract something—a kind of all–permeating wakefulness. Oh, I can't explain it! Who could? But its spiritual, not just a thing bred out of a condition, like fire, as you say, or electricity. It's a horrible thought of yours. Life's a kind of spiritual mystery—'

'Easy, my boy!' said the old doctor, laughing gently to himself. 'Or else I may be asking you to demonstrate the spiritual mystery of life of the limpet, or the crab, shall we say.' He grinned at me with ineffable perverseness. 'Anyway,' he continued, 'as I suppose you've all guessed, I've a yarn to tell you in support of my impression that life is no more a mystery or a miracle than fire or electricity. But, please to remember, gentlemen, that because we've succeeded in naming and making good use of these two forces, they're just as much mysteries, fundamentally as ever. And, anyway, the thing I'm going to tell you won't explain the mystery of life, but only give you one of my pegs on which I hang my feeling that life is as I have said, a force made manifest through conditions—that is to say, natural chemistry—and that it can take for its purpose and need, the most incredible and unlikely matter; for without matter it cannot come into existence—it cannot become manifest—'

'I don't agree with you, doctor,' I interrupted. 'Your theory would destroy all belief in life after death. It would—'

'Hush, sonny,' said the old man, with a quiet little smile of comprehension. 'Hark to what I've to say first; and, anyway, what objection have you to material life after death? And if you object to a material framework, I would still have you remember that I am speaking of life, as we understand the word in this our life. Now do be a quiet lad, or I'll never be done:

'It was when I was a young man, and that is a good many years ago, gentlemen. I had passed my examinations, but was so run down with overwork that it was decided that I had better take a trip to sea. I was by no means well off, and very glad in the end to secure a nominal post as doctor in the sailing passenger clipper running out to China.

'The name of the ship was the Bheospsé, and soon after I had got all my gear aboard she cast off, and we dropped down the Thames, and next day were well away out in the Channel.

'The captain's name was Gannington, a very decent man, though quite illiterate. The first mate, Mr Berlies, was a quiet, sternish, reserved man, very well–read. The second mate, Mr Selvern, was, perhaps, by birth and upbringing, the most socially cultured of the three, but he lacked the stamina and indomitable pluck of the two others. He was more of a sensitive, and emotionally and even mentally, the most alert man of the three.

'On our way out, we called at Madagascar, where we landed some of our passengers; then we ran eastward, meaning to call at North–West Cape; but about a hundred degrees east we encountered very dreadful weather, which carried away all our sails, and sprung the jibboom and foret'gallantmast.

'The storm carried us northward for several hundred miles, and when it dropped us finally, we found ourselves in a very bad state. The ship had been strained, and had taken some three feet of water through her seams; the maintopmast had been sprung, in addition to the jibboom and foret'gallantmast, two of our boats had gone, as also one of the pigstys, with three fine pigs, these latter having been washed overboard but some half–hour before the wind began to ease, which it did very quickly, though a very ugly sea ran for some hours after.

'The wind left us just before dark, and when morning came it brought splendid weather—a calm, mildly undulating sea, and a brilliant sun, with no wind. It showed us also that we were not alone, for about two miles away to the westward was another vessel, which Mr Selvern, the second mate, pointed out to me.

'That's a pretty rum–looking, packet, doctor,' he said, and handed me his glass.

'I looked through it at the other vessel, and saw what he meant; at least, I thought I did.

'Yes, Mr Selvern,' I said. 'She's got a pretty old–fashioned look about her.'

'He laughed at me in his pleasant way.

'It's easy to see you're not a sailor, doctor,' he remarked.

'There's a dozen rum things about her.

She's a derelict, and has been floating round, by the look of her, for many a score of years. Look at the shape of her counter, and the bows and cutwater. She's as old as the hills, as you might say, and ought to have gone down to Davy Jones a good while ago. Look at the growths on her, and the thickness of her standing rigging; that's all salt encrustations, I fancy, if you notice the white colour. She's been a small barque; but, don't you see, she's not a yard left aloft. They've all dropped out of the slings; everything rotted away; wonder the standing rigging hasn't gone, too. I wish the old man would let us take the boat and have a look at her. She'd be well worth it.'

'There seemed little chance, however, of this, for all hands were turned to and kept hard at it all day long repairing the damage to the masts and gear; and this took a long while, as you may think. Part of the time I gave a hand heaving on one of the deck capstans, for the exercise was good for my liver. Old Captain Gannington approved, and I persuaded him to come along and try some of the same medicine, which he did; and we got very chummy over the job.

'We got talking about the derelict, and he remarked

how lucky we were not to have run full tilt on to her in the darkness, for she lay right away to leeward of us, according, to the way that we had been drifting in the storm. He also was of the opinion that she had a strange look about her, and that she was pretty old; but on this latter point he plainly had far less knowledge than the second mate, for he was, as I have said, an illiterate man, and knew nothing of seacraft beyond what experience had taught him. He lacked the book knowledge which the second mate had of vessels previous to his day, which it appeared the derelict was.

'She's an old 'un, doctor,' was the extent of observations in this direction.

'Yet, when I mentioned to him that it would be interesting to go aboard and give her a bit of an overhaul, he nodded his head as if the idea had been already in his mind and accorded with his own inclinations.

'When the work's over, doctor,' he said. 'Can't spare the men now, ye know. Got to get all shipshape an' ready as smart as we can. But, we'll take my gig, an' go off in the second dog–watch. The glass is steady, an' it'll be a bit of gam for us.'

'That evening, after tea, the captain gave orders to clear the gig and get her overboard. The second mate was to come with us, and the skipper gave him word to see that two or three lamps were put into the boat, as it would soon fall dark. A little later we were pulling across the calmness of the sea with a crew of six at the oars, and making very good speed of it.

'Now, gentlemen, I have detailed to you with great exactness all the facts, both big and little, so that you can follow step by step each incident in this extraordinary affair, and I want you now to pay the closest attention. I was sitting in the stern–sheets with the second mate and the captain, who was steering, and as we drew nearer and nearer to the stranger I studied her with an ever–growing attention, as, indeed, did Captain Gannington and the second mate. She was, as you know, to the west–ward of us, and the sunset was making a great flame of red light to the back of her, so that she showed a little blurred and indistinct by reason of the halation of the light, which almost defeated the eye in any attempt to see her rotting spars and standing rigging, submerged, as they were, in the fiery glory of the sunset.

'It was because of this effect of the sunset that we had come quite close, comparatively, to the derelict before we saw that she was all surrounded by a sort of curious scum, the colour of which was difficult to decide upon by reason of the red light that was in the atmosphere, but which afterwards we discovered to be brown. This scum spread all about the old vessel for many hundreds of yards in a huge, irregular patch, a great stretch of which reached out to the eastward, upon the starboard side of the boat some score or so fathoms away.

'Queer stuff,' said Captain Gannington, leaning to the side and looking over. 'Something in the cargo as'as gone rotten, and worked out through 'er seams.'

''Look at her bows and stern,' said the second mate. 'Just look at the growth on her!'

'There were, as he said, great clumpings of strange–looking sea–fungi under the bows and the short counter astern. From the stump of her jibboom and her cutwater great beards of rime and marine growths hung downward into the scum that held her in. Her blank starboard side was presented to us—all a dead, dirtyish white, streaked and mottled vaguely with dull masses of heavier colour.

'There's a steam or haze rising off her,' said the second mate, speaking again. 'You can see it against the light. It keeps coming and going. Look!'

'I saw then what he meant—a faint haze or steam, either suspended above the old vessel or rising from her. And Captain Gannington saw it also.

'Spontaneous combustion!' he exclaimed. 'We'll 'ave to watch when we lift the 'atches, 'nless it's some poor devil that's got aboard of 'er. But that ain't likely.'

'We were now within a couple of hundred yards of the old derelict, and had entered into the brown scum. As it poured off the lifted oars I heard one of the men mutter to himself, 'Dam' treacle!' And, indeed, it was not something unlike it. As the boat continued to forge nearer and nearer to the old ship the scum grew thicker and thicker, so that, at last, it perceptibly slowed us.

'Give way, lads! Put some beef to it!' sang out Captain Gannington. And thereafter there was no sound except the panting of the men and the faint, reiterated suck, suck of the sullen brown scum upon the oars as the boat was forced ahead. As we went, I was conscious of a peculiar smell in the evening air, and whilst I had no doubt that the puddling of the scum by the oars made it rise, I could give no name to it; yet, in a way, it was vaguely familiar.

'We were now very close to the old vessel, and presently she was high about us against the dying light. The captain called out then to 'in with the bow oars and stand by with the boat–hook,' which was done.

'Aboard there! Ahoy! Aboard there! Ahoy!' shouted Captain Gannington; but there came no answer, only the dull sound his voice going lost into the open sea, each time he sung out.

'Ahoy! Aboard there! Ahoy!' he shouted time after time, but there was only the weary silence of the old hulk that answered us; and, somehow as he shouted, the while that I stared up half expectantly at her, a queer little sense of oppression, that amounted almost to nervousness, came upon me. It passed, but I remember how I was suddenly aware that it was growing dark. Darkness comes fairly rapidly in the tropics, though not so quickly as many fiction writers seem to think; but it was not that the coming dusk had perceptibly deepened in that brief time of only a few moments, but rather that my nerves had made me suddenly a little hypersensitive. I mention my state particularly, for I am not a nervy man normally, and my abrupt touch of nerves is significant, in the light of what happened.

'There's no one on board there!' said Captain Gannington. 'Give way, men!' For the boat's crew had instinctively rested on their oars, as the captain hailed the old craft. The men gave way again; and then the second mate called out excitedly, 'Why, look there, there's our pigsty! See, it's got Bheospsé painted on the end. It's drifted down here and the scum's caught it. What a blessed wonder!'

'It was, as he had said, our pigsty that had been washed overboard in the storm; and most extraordinary to come across it there.

'We'll tow it off with us, when we go,' said the captain, and shouted to the crew to get down to their oars; for they were hardly moving the boat, because the scum was so thick, close in around the old ship, that it literally clogged the boat from moving. I remember that it struck me, in a half–conscious sort of way, as curious that the pigsty, containing our three dead pigs, had managed to drift in so far unaided, whilst we could scarcely manage to force the boat in, now that we had come right into the scum. But the thought passed from my mind, for so many things happened within the next few minutes.

'The men managed to bring the boat in alongside, within a couple of feet of the derelict, and the man with the boat–hook hooked on.

'Ave ye got 'old there, forrard?' asked Captain Gannington.'

'Yes sir!' said the bowman; and as he spoke there came a queer noise of tearing.'

'What's that?' asked the Captain.'

'It's tore, sir. Tore clean away!' said the man, and his tone showed that he had received something of a shock.'

'Get a hold again, then!' said Captain Gannington irritably. 'You don't s'pose this packet was built yesterday! Shove the hook into the main chains' The man did so gingerly, as you might say, for it seemed to me, in the growing dusk, that he put no strain on to the hook, though, of course there was no need—you see the boat could not go very far of herself, in the stuff in which she was imbedded. I remember thinking this, also as I looked up at the bulging side of the old vessel. Then I heard Captain Gannington's voice:

'Lord, but she s old! An' what a colour, doctor! She don't half want paint, do she? Now then, somebody, one of them oars.' An oar was passed to him, and he leant it up against the ancient, bulging side; then he paused, and called to the second mate to light a couple of the lamps, and stand by to pass them up, for darkness had settled down now upon the sea.

'The second mate lit two of the lamps, and told one of the men to light a third, and keep it handy in the boat; then he stepped across, with a lamp in each hand, to where Captain Gannington stood by the oar against the side of the ship.

'Now, my lad,' said the captain to the man who had pulled stroke, 'up with you, an' we'll pass ye up the lamps.'

'The man jumped to obey, caught the oar, and put his weight upon it; and as he did so, something seemed to give way a little.

'Look!' cried out the second mate, and pointed, lamp in hand. 'It's sunk in!'

'This was true. The oar had made quite an indentation into the bulging, somewhat slimy side of the old vessel.

'Mould, I reckon,' said Captain Gannington, bending towards the derelict to look. Then to the man:

'Up you go, my lad, and be smart! Don't stand there waitin'!'

'At that the man, who had paused a moment as he felt the oar give beneath his weight began to shin' up, and in a few seconds he was aboard, and leant out over the rail for the lamps. These were passed up to him, and the captain called to him to steady the oar. Then Captain Gannington went, calling to me to follow, and after me the second mate.

'As the captain put his face over the rail, he gave a cry of astonishment.

'Mould, by gum! Mould—tons of it. Good lord!'

'As I heard him shout that I scrambled the more eagerly after him, and in a moment or two I was able to see what he meant—everywhere that the light from the two lamps struck there was nothing but smooth great masses and surfaces of a dirty white coloured mould. I climbed over the rail, with the second mate close behind, and stood upon the mould covered decks. There might have been no planking beneath the mould, for all that our feet could feel. It gave under our tread with a spongy, puddingy feel. It covered the deck furniture of the old ship, so that the shape of each article and fitment was often no more than suggested through it.

'Captain Gannington snatched a lamp from the man and the second mate reached for the other. They held the lamps high, and we all stared. It was most extraordinary, and somehow most abominable. I can think of no other word, gentlemen, that so much describes the predominant feeling that affected me at the moment.

'Good lord!' said Captain Gannington several times. 'Good lord!' But neither the second mate nor the man said anything, and, for my part I just stared, and at the same time began to smell a little at the air, for there was a vague odour of something half familiar, that somehow brought to me a sense of half–known fright.

'I turned this way and that, staring, as I have said. Here and there the mould was so heavy as to entirely disguise what lay beneath, converting the deck–fittings into indistinguishable mounds of mould all dirty–white and blotched and veined with irregular, dull, purplish markings.

'There was a strange thing about the mould which Captain Gannington drew attention to—it was that our feet did not crush into it and break the surface, as might have been expected, but merely indented it.

'Never seen nothin' like it before! Never!' said the captain after having stooped with his lamp to examine the mould under our feet. He stamped with his heel, and the mould gave out a dull, puddingy sound. He stooped again, with a quick movement, and stared, holding the lamp close to the deck. 'Blest if it ain't a reg'lar skin to it!'

'The second mate and the man and I all stooped and looked at it. The second mate progged it with his forefinger, and I remember I rapped it several times with my knuckles, listening to the dead sound it gave out, and noticing the close, firm texture of the mould.

'Dough!' the second mate. 'It's just like blessed dough! Pouf!' He stood up with a quick movement. 'I could fancy it stinks a bit,' he said.

'As he said this I knew, suddenly, what the familiar thing was in the vague odour that hung about us—it was that the smell had something animal–like in it; something of the same smell, only heavier, that you would smell in any place that is infested with mice. I began to look about with a sudden very real uneasiness. There might be vast numbers of hungry rats aboard. They might prove exceedingly dangerous, if in a starving condition; yet, as you will understand, somehow I hesitated to put forward my idea as a reason for caution, it was too fanciful.

'Captain Gannington had begun to go aft along the mould–covered main–deck with the second mate, each of them holding their lamps high up, so as to cast a good light about the vessel. I turned quickly and followed them, the man with me keeping close to my heels, and plainly uneasy. As we went, I became aware that there was a feeling of moisture in the air, and I remembered the slight mist, or smoke, above the hulk, which had made Captain Gannington suggest spontaneous combustion in explanation.

'And always, as we went, there was that vague, animal smell; suddenly I found myself wishing we were well away from the old vessel.

'Abruptly, after a few paces, the captain stopped and pointed at a row of mould–hidden shapes on each side of the maindeck. 'Guns,' he said. 'Been a privateer in the old days, I guess—maybe worse! We'll 'ave a look below, doctor; there may be something worth touchin'. She's older than I thought. Mr Selvern thinks she's about two hundred years old; but I scarce think it.'

'We continued our way aft, and I remember that I found myself walking as lightly and gingerly as possible, as if I were subconsciously afraid of treading through the rotten, mould–hid decks. I think the others had a touch of the same feeling, from the way that they walked. Occasionally the soft stuff would grip our heels, releasing them with a little sullen suck.

'The captain forged somewhat ahead of the second mate; and I know that the suggestion he had made himself, that perhaps there might be something below worth carrying away, had stimulated his imagination. The second mate was, however, beginning to feel somewhat the same way that I did; at least I have that impression. I think, if it had not been for what I might truly describe as Captain Gannington's sturdy courage, we should all of us have just gone back over the side very soon, for there was most certainly an unwholesome feeling abroad that made one feel queerly lacking in pluck; and you will soon see that this feeling was justified.

'Just as the captain reached the few mould–covered steps leading up on to the short half–poop, I was suddenly aware that the feeling of moisture in the air had grown very much more definite. It was perceptible now, intermittently, as a sort of thin, moist, fog–like vapour, that came and went oddly, and seemed to make the decks a little indistinct to the view, this time and that. Once an odd puff of it beat up suddenly from somewhere, and caught me in the face, carrying a queer, sickly, heavy odour with it that somehow frightened me strangely with a suggestion of a waiting and half–comprehended danger.

'We had followed Captain Gannington up the three

mould covered steps, and now went slowly along the raised after–deck. By the mizzenmast Captain Gannington paused, and held his lantern near to it. 'My word, mister,' he said to the second mate, 'it's fair thickened up with mould! Why, I'll g'antee it's close on four foot thick.' He shone the light down to where it met the deck. 'Good lord!' he said. 'Look at the sea–lice on it!' I stepped up, and it was as he had said; the sea–lice were thick upon it, some of them huge, not less than the size of large beetles, and all a clear, colourless shade, like water, except where there were little spots of grey on them.

'I've never seen the like of them, 'cept on a live cod,' said Captain Gannington, in an extremely puzzled voice. 'My word! But they're whoppers!' Then he passed on; but a few paces farther aft he stopped again, and held his lamp near to the mould–hidden deck.

'Lord bless me, doctor,' he called out, in a low voice, 'did ye ever see the like of that? Why, it's a foot long, if it's a hinch!'

'I stooped over his shoulder, and saw what he meant; it was a clear, colourless creature about a foot long, and about eight inches high, with a curved back that was extraordinarily narrow. As we stared, all in a group, it gave a queer little flick, and was gone.

'Jumped!' said the captain. 'Well, if that ain't a giant of all the sea–lice that ever I've seen. I guess it's jumped twenty foot clear.' He straightened his back, and scratched his head a moment, swinging the lantern this way and that with the other hand, and staring about us. 'Wot are they doin' aboard 'ere?' he said. 'You'll see 'em—little things—on fat cod an' such–like. I'm blowed, doctor, if I understand.'

'He held his lamp towards a big mound of the mould that occupied part of the after portion of the low poop–deck, a little foreside of where there came a two–foot high 'break' to a kind of second and loftier poop, that ran away aft to the taffrail. The mound was pretty big, several feet across, and more than a yard high. Captain Gannington walked up to it.

'I reck'n this's the scuttle,' he remarked, and gave it a heavy kick. The only result was a deep indentation into the huge, whiteish hump of mould, as if he had driven his foot into a mass of some doughy substance.

Yet I am not altogether correct in saying that this was the only result, for a certain other thing happened.

From the place made by the captain's foot there came a sudden gush of a purplish fluid, accompanied by a peculiar smell, that was, and was not, half familiar. Some of the mould–like substance had stuck to the toe of the captain's boot, and from this likewise there issued a sweat, as it were, of the same colour.

'Well?' said Captain Gannington, in surprise, and drew back his foot to make another kick at the hump of mould. But he paused at an exclamation from the second mate:

'Don't sir,' said the second mate.

'I glanced at him, and the light from Captain Gannington's lamp showed me that his face had a bewildered, half–frightened look, as if he were suddenly and unexpectedly half afraid of something, and as if his tongue had given away his sudden fright, without any intention on his part to speak. The captain also turned and stared at him.

'Why, mister?' he asked, in a somewhat puzzled voice, through which there sounded just the vaguest hint of annoyance. 'We've got to shift this muck, if we're to get below.'

'I looked at the second mate, and it seemed to me that, curiously enough he was listening less to the captain than to some other sound. Suddenly he said, in a queer voice, 'Listen, everybody!'

'Yet we heard nothing, beyond the faint murmur of the men talking together in the boat alongside.

'I don't, hear nothing,' said Captain Gannington, after a short pause. 'Do you, doctor?'

'No,' I said.

'Wot was it you thought you heard?' the captain, turning again to the second mate. But the second mate shook his head in a curious, almost irritable way, as if the captain's question interrupted his listening.

Captain Gannington stared a moment at him, then held his lantern up and glanced about him almost uneasily. I know I felt a queer sense of strain. But the light showed nothing beyond the greyish dirty–white of the mould in all directions.

'Mister Selvern,' said the captain, at last, looking at him, 'don't get fancying, things. Get hold of your bloomin' self. Ye know ye heard nothin'?'

'I'm quite sure I heard something, sir,' said the second mate. 'I seemed to hear—' He broke off sharply, and appeared to listen with an almost painful intensity.

'What did it sound like?' I asked.

'It's all right, doctor,' said Captain Gannington, laughing gently. 'Ye can give him a tonic when we get back. I'm goin' to shift this stuff.' He drew back, and kicked for the second time at the ugly mass which he took to hide the companionway. The result of his kick was startling, for the whole thing wobbled sloppily, like a mound of unhealthy–looking jelly.

'He drew his foot out of it quickly, and took a step backward, staring, and holding his lamp towards it.

'By gum,' he said, and it was plain that he was generally startled, 'the blessed thing's gone soft!'

'The man had run back several steps from the suddenly flaccid mound, and looking horribly frightened. Though of what, I am sure he had not the least idea. The second mate stood where he was, and stared.

For my part, I know I had a most hideous uneasiness upon me. The captain continued to hold his light towards the wobbling mound and stare.

'It's gone squashy all through,' he said. 'There's no scuttle there. There's no bally woodwork inside that lot! Phoo! What a rum smell!'

'He walked round to the after side of the strange mound, to see whether there might be some signs of an opening, into the hull at the back of the great heap of mould–stuff. And then:

'Listen!' said the second mate again, in the strangest sort of voice.

'Captain Gannington straightened himself upright, and there succeeded a pause of the most intense quietness, in which there was not even the hum of talk from the men alongside in the boat. We all heard it—a kind of dull, soft thud, thud, thud, thud, somewhere in the hull under us, yet so vague as to make me half doubtful I heard it, only that the others did so, too.

'Captain Gannington turned suddenly to where the man stood.

'Tell them—' he began. But the fellow cried out something, and pointed. There had come a strange intensity into his somewhat unemotional face, so that the captain's glance followed his action instantly. I stared also as you may think. It was the great mound at which the man was pointing. I saw what he meant. From the two gapes made in the mould–like stuff by Captain Gannington's boot, the purple fluid was jetting out in a queerly regular fashion, almost as if it were being forced out by a pump. My word! But I stared! And even as I stared a larger jet squirted out, and splashed as far as the man, spattering his boots and trouser legs.

'The fellow had been pretty nervous before, in a stolid, ignorant sort of way, and his funk had been growing steadily; but at this he simply let out a yell, and turned about to run. He paused an instant, as if a sudden fear of the darkness that held the decks, between him and the boat, had taken him. He snatched at the second mate's lantern, tore it out of his hand, and plunged heavily away over the vile stretch of mould.

'Mr Selvern, the second mate, said not a word; he was just staring, staring at the strange–smelling twin–streams of dull purple that were jetting out from the wobbling mound. Captain Gannington, however, roared an order to the man to come back, but the man plunged on and on across the mould, his feet seeming to be clogged by the stuff, as if it had grown suddenly soft. He zigzagged as he ran, the lantern swaying, in wild circles as he wrenched his feet free with a constant plop, plop; and I could hear his frightened gasps even from where I stood.

'Come back with that lamp!' roared the captain again; but still the man took no notice.

'And Captain Gannington was silent an instant, his lips working in a queer, inarticulate fashion, as if he were stunned momentarily by the very violence of his anger at the man's insubordination. And in the silence I heard the sounds again—thud, thud, thud, thud! Quite distinctly now, beating, it seemed suddenly to me, right down under my feet, but deep.

'I stared down at the mould on which I was standing, with a quick, disgusting sense of the terrible all about me; then I looked at the captain, and tried to say something, without appearing frightened. I saw that he had turned again to the mound, and all the anger had gone out of his face. He had his lamp out towards the mound, and was listening. There was another moment of absolute silence, at least, I knew that I was not conscious of any sound at all in all the world, except that extraordinary thud, thud, thud, thud, down somewhere in the huge bulk under us.

'The captain shifted his feet with a sudden, nervous movement, and as he lifted them the mould went plop, plop! He looked quickly at me, trying to smile, as if he were not thinking anything very much about it.

'What do you make of it, doctor?' he said.

'I think—' I began. But the second mate interrupted with a single word, his voice pitched a little high, in a tone that made us both stare instantly at him.

'Look!' he said, and pointed at the mound. The thing was all of a slow quiver. A strange ripple ran outward from it, along the deck, like you will see a ripple run inshore out of a calm sea. It reached a mound a little foreside of us, which I had supposed to be the cabin skylight, and in a moment the second mound sank nearly level with the surrounding decks, quivering floppily in a most extraordinary fashion. A sudden quick tremor took the mould right under the second mate, and he gave out a hoarse little cry, and held his arms out on each side of him, to keep his balance. The tremor in the mould spread, and

Captain Gannington swayed, and spread out his feet with a sudden curse of fright. The second mate jumped across to him, and caught him by the wrist.

'The boat, sir!' he said, saying the very thing that I had lacked the pluck to say. 'For God's sake—'

'But he never finished, for a tremendous hoarse scream cut off his words. They hove themselves round and looked. I could see without turning. The man who had run from us was standing in the waist of the ship, about a fathom from the starboard bulwarks. He was swaying from side to side, and screaming, in a dreadful fashion. He appeared to be trying to lift his feet, and the light from his swaying lantern showed an almost incredible sight. All about him the mould was in active movement. His feet had sunk out of sight.

The stuff appeared to be lapping at his legs and abruptly his bare flesh showed. The hideous stuff had rent his trouser–leg away as if it were paper. He gave out a simply sickening scream, and, with a vast effort, wrenched one leg free. It was partly destroyed. The next instant he pitched face downward, and the stuff heaped itself upon him, as if it were actually alive, with a dreadful, severe life. It was simply infernal. The man had gone from sight. Where he had fallen was now a writhing, elongated mound, in constant and horrible increase, as the mould appeared to move towards it in strange ripples from all sides.

'Captain Gannington and the second mate were stone silent, in amazed and incredulous horror, but I had begun to reach towards a grotesque and terrific conclusion, both helped and hindered by my professional training.

'From the men in the boat alongside there was a loud shouting. and I saw two of their faces appear suddenly above the rail. They showed clearly a moment in the light from the lamp which the man had snatched from Mr Selvern; for, strangely enough, this lamp was standing upright and unharmed on the deck, a little way foreside of that dreadful, elongated, growing mound, that still swayed and writhed with an incredible horror. The lamp rose and fell on the passing ripples of the mould, just—for all the world—as you will see a boat rise and fall on little swells. It is of some interest to me now, psychologically, to remember how that rising and falling lantern brought home to me more than anything the incomprehensible dreadful strangeness of it all.

'The men's faces disappeared with sudden yells, as if they had slipped, or been suddenly hurt; and there was a fresh uproar of shouting from the boat. The men were calling to us to come away—to come away. In the same instant I felt my left boot drawn suddenly and forcibly downward, with a horrible, painful grip. I wrenched it free, with a yell of angry fear. Forrard of us, I saw that the vile surface was all amove, and abruptly I found myself shouting in a queer, frightened voice, 'The boat, captain! The boat, captain!'

'Captain Gannington stared round at me, over his right shoulder, in a peculiar, dull way, that told me he was utterly dazed with bewilderment and the incomprehensibleness of it all. I took a quick, clogged, nervous step towards him, and gripped his arm, and shook it fiercely. 'The boat!'

I shouted at him. 'The boat! For God's sake, tell the men to bring the boat aft!'

'Then the mound must have drawn his feet down, for abruptly he bellowed fiercely with terror, his momentary apathy giving place to furious energy. His thickset, vastly muscular body doubled and writhed with his enormous effort, and he struck out madly dropping the lantern. He tore his feet free, something ripping as he did so. The reality and necessity of the situation had come upon him brutishly real, and he was roaring to the men in the boat, 'Bring the boat aft! Bring 'er aft! Bring 'er aft!' The second mate and I were shouting the same thing madly.

'For God's sake, be smart, lads!' roared the captain, and stooped quickly for his lamp, which still burned. His feet were gripped again, and he hove them out, blaspheming breathlessly, and leaping a yard high with his effort. Then he made a run for the side, wrenching his feet free at each step. In the same instant the second mate cried out something, and grabbed at the captain.

'It's got hold of my feet! It's got hold of my feet!' he screamed. His feet, had disappeared up to his boot–tops, and Captain Gannington caught him round the waist with his powerful left arm, gave a mighty heave, and the next instant had him free; but both his boot–soles had gone. For my part, I jumped madly from foot to foot, to avoid the plucking of the mould; and suddenly I made a run for the ship's side. But before I could get there, a queer gape came in the mould between us and the side, at least a couple of feet wide, and how deep I don't know. It closed up in an instant, and all the mould where the cape had been vent into a sort of flurry of horrible ripplings, so that I ran back from it; for I did not dare to put my foot upon it. Then the captain was shouting to me:

'Aft, doctor! Aft, doctor! This way, doctor! Run!' I saw then that he had passed me, and was up on the after raised portion of the poop. He had the second mate, thrown like a sack, all loose and quiet, over his left shoulder; for Mr Selvern had fainted, and his long legs flogged limp and helpless against the captain's massive knees as he ran. I saw, with a queer, unconscious noting of minor details, how the torn soles of the second mate's boots flapped and jigged as the captain staggered aft.

'Boat ahoy! Boat ahoy! Boat ahoy!' shouted the captain;

and then I was beside him, shouting also. The men were answering with loud yells of encouragement, and it was plain they were working desperately to force the boat aft through the thick scum about the ship.

'We reached the ancient, mould–hid taffrail, and slewed about breathlessly in the half–darkness to see what was happening. Captain Gannington had left his lantern by the big mound when he picked up the second mate; and as we stood, gasping we discovered suddenly that all the mould between us and the light was full of movement. Yet, the part on which we stood, for about six or eight feet forrard of us, was still firm.

'Every couple of seconds we shouted to the men to hasten, and they kept on calling to us that they would be with us in an instant. And all the time we watched the deck of that dreadful hulk, feeling, for my part, literally sick with mad suspense, and ready to jump overboard into that filthy scum all about us.

'Down somewhere in the huge bulk of the ship there was all the time that extraordinary dull, ponderous thud, thud, thud, thud growing ever louder. I seemed to feel the whole hull of the derelict, beginning to quiver and thrill with each dull beat. And to me, with the grotesque and hideous suspicion of what made that noise, it was at once the most dreadful and incredible sound I have ever heard.

'As we waited desperately for the boat, I scanned incessantly so much of the grey white bulk as the lamp showed. The whole of the decks seemed to be in strange movement. Forrard of the lamp, I could see indistinctly the moundings of the mould swaying and nodding hideously beyond the circle of the brightest rays. Nearer, and full in the glow of the lamp, the mound which should have indicated the skylight, was swelling steadily. There were ugly, purple veinings on it, and as it swelled, it seemed to me that the veinings and mottlings on it were becoming plainer, rising as though embossed upon it, like you will see the veins stand out on the body of a powerful, full–blooded horse. It was most extraordinary. The mound that we had supposed to cover the companionway had sunk flat with the surrounding mould, and I could not see that it jetted out any more of the purplish fluid.

'A quaking movement of the mound began away forrard of the lamp, and came flurrying away aft towards us, and at the sight of that I climbed up on to the spongy–feeling taffrail, and yelled afresh for the boat. The men answered with a shout, which told me they were nearer, but the beastly scum was so thick that it was evidently a fight to move the boat at all. Beside me, Captain Gannington was shaking the second mate furiously, and the man stirred and began to moan. The captain shook him again, 'Wake up! Wake up, mister!' he shouted.

'The second mate staggered out of the captain's arms, and collapsed suddenly, shrieking: 'My feet! Oh, God! My feet!' The captain and I lugged him off the mound, and got him into a sitting position upon the taffrail, where he kept up a continual moaning.

'Hold 'im, doctor,' said the captain. And whilst I did so, he ran forrard a few yards, and peered down over the starboard quarter rail. 'For God's sake, be smart, lads! Be smart! Be smart!' he shouted down to the men, and they answered him, breathless, from close at hand, yet still too far away for the boat to be any use to us on the instant.

'I was holding the moaning, half-unconscious officer, and staring forrard along the poop decks. The flurrying of the mould was coming aft, slowly and noiselessly. And then, suddenly, I saw something closer:

'Look out, captain!' I shouted. And even as I shouted, the mould near to him gave a sudden, peculiar slobber. I had seen a ripple stealing towards him through the mould. He gave an enormous, clumsy leap, and landed near to us on the sound part of the mould, but the movement followed him. He turned and faced it, swearing fiercely. All about his feet there came abruptly little gapings, which made horrid sucking noises. 'Come back, captain!' I yelled. 'Come back, quick!' As I shouted, a ripple came at his feet—lipping at them; and he stamped insanely at it, and leaped back, his boot torn half off his foot. He swore madly with pain and anger, and jumped swiftly for the taffrail.

'Come on, doctor! Over we go!' he called. Then he remembered the filthy scum, and hesitated, and roared out desperately to the men to hurry. I stared down, also.

'The second mate?' I said.

'I'll take charge doctor,' said Captain Gannington, and caught hold of Mr Selvern. As he spoke, I thought I saw something beneath us, outlined against the scum. I leaned out over the stern, and peered.

There was something under the port–quarter.

'There's something down there, captain!' I called, and pointed in the darkness. He stooped far over, and stared.

'A boat, by gum! A boat!' he yelled, and began to wriggle swiftly along the taffrail, dragging the second mate after him. I followed. 'A boat it is, sure!' he exclaimed a few moments later, and, picking up the second mate clear of the rail, he hove him down into the boat, where he fell with a crash into the bottom.

'Over ye go, doctor!' he yelled at me, and pulled me bodily off the rail and dropped me after the officer. As he did so, I felt the whole of the ancient, spongy rail give a peculiar, sickening quiver, and begin to wobble. I fell on to the second mate, and the captain came after, almost in the same instant, but, fortunately, he landed clear of us, on to the fore thwart, which broke under his weight, with a loud crack and splintering of wood.

'Thank God!' I heard him mutter. 'Thank God! I guess that was a mighty near thing to going to Hades.'

'He struck a match, just as I got to my feet, and between us we got the second mate straightened out on one of the after fore–and–aft thwarts. We shouted to the men in the boat, telling them where we were, and saw the light of their lantern shining round the starboard counter of the derelict. They called back to us to tell us they were doing their best, and then, whilst we waited, Captain Gannington struck another match, and began to overhaul the boat we had dropped into. She was a modern, two–bowed boat, and on the stern there was painted 'Cyclone, Glasgow.' She was in pretty fair condition, and had evidently drifted into the scum and been held by it.

'Captain Gannington struck several matches, and went forrard towards the derelict. Suddenly he called to me, and I jumped over the thwarts to him. 'Look, doctor,' he said, and I saw what he meant—a mass of bones up in the bows of the boat. I stooped over them, and looked; there were the bones of at least three people, all mixed together in an extraordinary fashion, and quite clean and dry. I had a sudden thought concerning the bones, but I said nothing, for my thought was vague in some ways, and concerned the grotesque and incredible suggestion that had come to me as to the cause of that ponderous, dull thud, thud, thud thud, that beat on so infernally within the hull, and was plain to hear even now that we had got off the vessel herself. And all the while, you know, I had a sick, horrible mental picture of that frightful, wriggling mound aboard the hulk.

'As Captain Gannington struck a final match, I saw something that sickened me and the captain saw it in the same instant. The match went out, and he fumbled clumsily for another, and struck it. We saw the thing again. We had not been mistaken. A great lip of grey–white was protruding in over the edge of the boat—a great lappet of the mould was coming stealthily towards us—a live mass of the very hull itself! And suddenly Captain Gannington yelled out in so many words the grotesque and incredible thing I was thinking: 'She's alive!'

'I never heard such a sound of comprehension and terror in a man's voice. The very horrified assurance of it made actual to me the thing that before had only lurked in my subconscious mind. I knew he was right; I knew that the explanation my reason and my training both repelled and reached towards was the true one. Oh, I wonder whether anyone can possibly understand our feelings in that moment? The unmitigated horror of it and the incredibleness!

'As the light of the match burned up fully, I saw that the mass of living matter coming towards us was streaked and veined with purple, the veins standing out, enormously distended. The whole thing quivered continuously to each ponderous thud, thud, thud, thud, of that gargantuan organ that pulsed within the huge grey–white bulk. The flame of the match reached the captain's fingers, and there came to me a little sickly whiff of burned flesh, but he seemed unconscious of any pain. Then the flame went out in a brief sizzle, yet at the last moment I had seen an extraordinary raw look become visible upon the end of that monstrous, protruding lappet. It had become dewed with a hideous, purplish sweat. And with the darkness there came a sudden charnel–like stench.

'I heard the matchbox split in Captain Gannington's hands as he wrenched it open. Then he swore, in a queer frightened voice, for he had come to the end of his matches. He turned clumsily in the darkness, and tumbled over the nearest thwart, in his eagerness to get to the stern of the boat; and I after him. For we knew that thing was coming towards us through the darkness, reaching over that piteous mingled heap of human bones all jumbled together in the bows. We shouted madly to the men, and for answer saw the bows of the boat emerge dimly into view round the starboard counter of the derelict.

'Thank God!' I gasped out. But Captain Gannington roared to them to show a light. Yet this they could not do, for the lamp had just been stepped on in their desperate efforts to force the boat round to us.

'Quick! Quick!' I shouted.

'For God's sake, be smart, men!' roared the captain.

'And both of us faced the darkness under the port–counter, out of which we knew—but could not see—the thing was coming to us.

'An oar! Smart, now—pass me an oar!' shouted the captain; and reached out his hands through the gloom towards the on–coming boat. I saw a figure stand up in the bows, and hold something out to us across the intervening yards of scum. Captain Gannington swept his hands through the darkness, and encountered it.

'I've got it! Let go there!' he said, in a quick, tense voice.

'In the same instant the boat we were in was pressed over suddenly to starboard by some tremendous weight. Then I heard the captain shout, 'Duck y'r head, doctor!' And directly afterwards he swung the heavy, fourteen–foot oar round his head, and struck into the darkness.

There came a sudden squelch, and he struck again, with a savage grunt of fierce energy. At the second blow the boat righted with a slow movement, and directly afterwards the other boat bumped gently into ours.

'Captain Gannington dropped the oar, and, springing across to the second mate, hove him up off the thwart, and pitched him with knee and arms clear in over the bows among the men; then he shouted to me to follow, which I did, and he came after me, bringing the oar with him. We carried the second mate aft, and the captain shouted to the men to back the boat a little; then they got her bows clear of the boat we had just left, and so headed out through the scum for the open sea.

'Where's Tom 'Arrison?' gasped one of the men, in the midst of his exertions. He happened to be Tom Harrison's particular chum, and Captain Gannington answered him briefly enough:

'Dead! Pull! Don't talk!'

'Now, difficult as it had been to force the boat through the scum to our rescue, the difficulty to get clear seemed tenfold. After some five minutes pulling, the boat seemed hardly to have moved a fathom, if so much, and a quite dreadful fear took me afresh, which one of the panting men put suddenly into words,

'It's got us!' he gasped out. 'Same as poor Tom!' It was the man who had inquired where Harrison was.

'Shut y'r mouth an' pull!' roared the captain. And so another few minutes passed. Abruptly, it seemed to me that the dull, ponderous thud, thud, thud, thud came more plainly through the dark, and I stared intently over the stern. I sickened a little, for I could almost swear that the dark mass of the monster was actually nearer—that it was coming nearer to us through the darkness. Captain Gannington must have had the same thought, for, after a brief look into the darkness, he jumped forrard, and began to double–bank the stroke–oar.

'Get forrid under the oars, doctor,' he said to me rather breathlessly. 'Get in the bows, an' see if you can't free the stuff a bit round the bows.'

'I did as he told me, and a minute later I was in the bows of the boat, puddling the scum from side to side, and trying to break up the viscid, clinging muck. A heavy almost animal–like smell rose off it, and all the air seemed full of the deadening, heavy smell. I shall never find words to tell anyone on earth the whole horror of it all—the threat that seemed to hang in the very air around us, and but a little astern that incredible thing, coming, as I firmly believed, nearer, and scum holding us, like half–melted glue.

'The minutes passed in a deadly, eternal fashion, and I kept staring back astern into the darkness but never ceasing to puddle that filthy scum, striking at it and switching it from side to side until I sweated.

'Abruptly Captain Gannington sang out: We're gaining, lads. Pull!' And I felt the boat forge ahead perceptibly, as they gave way with renewed hope and energy. There was soon no doubt of it, for presently that hideous thud, thud, thud, thud had grown quite dim and vague somewhere astern and I could no longer see the derelict, for the night had come down tremendously dark and all the sky was thick, overset with heavy clouds. As we drew nearer and nearer to the edge of the scum, the boat moved more and more perceptibly, until suddenly we emerged with a clean, sweet, fresh sound into the open sea.

'Thank God!' I said aloud, and drew in the boathook, and made my way aft again to where Captain Gannington now sat once more at the tiller. I saw him looking anxiously up at the sky and across to where the lights of our vessel burned, and again he would seem to listen intently, so that I found myself listening also.

'What's that, Captain?' I said sharply; for it seemed to me that I heard a sound far astern, something, between a queer whine and a low whistling. 'What's that?'

'It's wind, doctor.' he said in a low voice. 'I wish to God we were aboard.' Then to the men:

'Pull! Put y'r backs into it, or ye'll never put y'r teeth through good bread again!' The men obeyed nobly, and we reached the vessel safely, and had the boat safely stowed before the storm came, which it did in a furious white smother out of the west. I could see it for some minutes beforehand, tearing the sea in the gloom into a wall of phosphorescent foam; and as it came nearer, that peculiar whining, piping sound grew louder and louder, until it was like a vast steam whistle rushing towards us. And when it did come, we got it very heavy indeed, so that the morning showed us nothing but a welter of white seas, with that grim derelict many a score of miles away in the smother, lost as utterly as our hearts could wish to lose her.

'When I came to examine the second mate's feet, I found them in a very extraordinary condition. The soles of them had the appearance of having been partly digested. I know of no other word that so exactly describes their condition, and the agony the man suffered must have been dreadful.

'Now,' concluded the doctor, 'that is what I call a case in point. If we could know exactly what the old vessel had originally been loaded with, and the juxtaposition of the various articles of her cargo, plus the heat and time she had endured, plus one or two other only guessable quantities, we should have solved the chemistry of the life–force, gentlemen. Not necessarily the origin, mind you; but, at least, we should have taken a big step on the way. I've often regretted that gale, you know—in a way, that is, in a way. It was a most amazing discovery, but at the same time I had nothing but thankfulness to be rid of it. A most amazing chance. I often think of the way the monster woke out of its torpor. And that scum! The dead pigs caught in it! I fancy that was a grim kind of a net, gentlemen. It caught many things. It—' The old doctor sighed and nodded.

'If I could have had her bill of lading,' he said, his eyes full of regret. 'If—It might have told me something to help. But, anyway—' He began to fill his pipe again. 'I suppose,' he ended, looking round at us gravely, 'I s'pose we humans are an ungrateful lot of beggars at the best! But—but, what a chance? What a chance, eh?'

Jules Verne

(1828-1905)

Jules Verne (1828-1905) was an influential French novelist widely recognized as a pioneer of the science fiction genre. Among his most acclaimed works are *Twenty Thousand Leagues Under the Sea (1870), Journey to the Center of the Earth (1864), and Around the World in Eighty Days (1872).*

Michel Verne

(1861-1925)

Jules Verne's son who edited and completed several of his father's works after his death. He also wrote his own science fiction stories, though these were often published under his father's name to increase sales.

In The Year 2889

Jules Verne and Michel Verne

IN THE YEAR 2889.

Little though they seem to think of it, the people of this twenty–ninth century live continually in fairyland. Surfeited as they are with marvels, they are indifferent in presence of each new marvel. To them all seems natural. Could they but duly appreciate the refinements of civilization in our day; could they but compare the present with the past, and so better comprehend the advance we have made! How much fairer they would find our modern towns, with populations amounting sometimes to 10,000,000 souls; their streets 300 feet wide, their houses 1000 feet in height; with a temperature the same in all seasons; with their lines of aërial locomotion crossing the sky in every direction! If they would but picture to themselves the state of things that once existed, when through muddy streets rumbling boxes on wheels, drawn by horses—yes, by horses!—were the only means of conveyance. Think of the railroads of the olden time, and you will be able to appreciate the pneumatic tubes through which today one travels at the rate of 1000 miles an hour. Would not our contemporaries prize the telephone and the telephote more highly if they had not forgotten the telegraph?

Singularly enough, all these transformations rest upon principles which were perfectly familiar to our remote ancestors, but which they disregarded. Heat, for instance, is as ancient as man himself; electricity was known 3000 years ago, and steam 1100 years ago. Nay, so early as ten centuries ago it was known that the differences between the several chemical and physical forces depend on the mode of vibration of the etheric particles, which is for each specifically different. When at last the kinship of all these forces was discovered, it is simply astounding that 500 years should still have to elapse before men could analyze and describe the several modes of vibration that constitute these differences. Above all, it is singular that the mode of reproducing these forces directly from one another, and of reproducing one without the others, should have remained undiscovered till less than a hundred years ago. Nevertheless, such was the course of events, for it was not till the year 2792 that the famous Oswald Nier made this great discovery.

Truly was he a great benefactor of the human race. His admirable discovery led to many another. Hence is sprung a pleiad of inventors, its brightest star being our great Joseph Jackson. To Jackson we are indebted for those wonderful instruments the new accumulators. Some of these absorb and condense the living force contained in the sun's rays; others, the electricity stored in our globe; others again, the energy coming from whatever source, as a waterfall, a stream, the winds, etc. He, too, it was that invented the transformer, a more wonderful contrivance still, which takes the living force from the accumulator, and, on the simple pressure of a button, gives it back to space in whatever form may be desired, whether as heat, light, electricity, or mechanical force, after having first obtained from it the work required. From the day when these two instruments were contrived is to be dated the era of true progress. They have put into the hands of man a power that is almost infinite. As for their applications, they are numberless. Mitigating the rigors of winter, by giving back to the atmosphere the surplus heat stored up during the summer, they have revolutionized agriculture. By supplying motive power for aërial navigation, they have given to commerce a mighty impetus. To them we are indebted for the continuous production of electricity without batteries or dynamos, of light without combustion or incandescence, and for an unfailing supply of mechanical energy for all the needs of industry.

Yes, all these wonders have been wrought by the accumulator and the transformer. And can we not to them also trace, indirectly, this latest wonder of all, the great 'Earth Chronicle' building in 253d Avenue, which was dedicated the other day? If George Washington Smith, the founder of the Manhattan 'Chronicle,' should come back to life today, what would he think were he to be told that this palace of marble and gold belongs to his remote descendant, Fritz Napoleon Smith, who, after thirty generations have come and gone, is owner of the same newspaper which his ancestor established!

For George Washington Smith's newspaper has lived generation after generation, now passing out of the family, anon coming back to it. When, 200 years ago, the political center of the United States was transferred from Washington to Centropolis, the newspaper followed the government and assumed the name of Earth Chronicle. Unfortunately, it was unable to maintain itself at the high level of its name. Pressed on all sides by rival journals of a more modern type, it was continually in danger of collapse. Twenty years ago its subscription list contained but a few hundred thousand names, and then Mr Fritz Napoleon Smith bought it for a mere trifle, and originated telephonic journalism.

Every one is familiar with Fritz Napoleon Smith's system—a system made possible by the enormous development of telephony during the last hundred years. Instead of being printed, the Earth Chronicle is every morning spoken to subscribers, who, in interesting conversations with reporters, statesmen, and scientists, learn the news of the day. Furthermore, each subscriber owns a phonograph, and to this instrument he leaves the task of gathering the news whenever he happens not to be in a mood to listen directly himself. As for purchasers of single copies, they can at a very trifling cost learn all that is in the paper of the day at any of the innumerable phonographs set up nearly everywhere.

Fritz Napoleon Smith's innovation galvanized the old newspaper. In the course of a few years the number of subscribers grew to be 85,000,000, and Smith's wealth went on growing, till now it reaches the almost unimaginable figure of $10,000,000,000. This lucky hit has enabled him to erect his new building, a vast edifice with four façades, each 3,250 feet in length, over which proudly floats the hundred-starred flag of the Union. Thanks to the same lucky hit, he is today king of newspaperdom; indeed, he would be king of all the Americans, too, if Americans could ever accept a king. You do not believe it? Well, then, look at the plenipotentiaries of all nations and our own ministers themselves crowding about his door, entreating his counsels, begging for his approbation, imploring the aid of his all–powerful organ. Reckon up the number of scientists and artists that he supports, of inventors that he has under his pay.

Yes, a king is he. And in truth his is a royalty full of burdens. His labors are incessant, and there is no doubt at all that in earlier times any man would have succumbed under the overpowering stress of the toil which Mr Smith has to perform. Very fortunately for him, thanks to the progress of hygiene, which, abating all the old sources of unhealthfulness, has lifted the mean of human life from 37 up to 52 years, men have stronger constitutions now than heretofore. The discovery of nutritive air is still in the future, but in the meantime men today consume food that is compounded and prepared according to scientific principles, and they breathe an atmosphere freed from the micro–organisms that formerly used to swarm in it; hence they live longer than their forefathers and know nothing of the innumerable diseases of olden times.

Nevertheless, and not with standing these considerations, Fritz Napoleon Smith's mode of life may well astonish one. His iron constitution is taxed to the utmost by the heavy strain that is put upon it. Vain the attempt to estimate the amount of labor he undergoes; an example alone can give an idea of it. Let us then go about with him for one day as he attends to his multifarious concernments. What day? That matters little; it is the same every day. Let us then take at random September 25th of this present year 2889.

This morning Mr Fritz Napoleon Smith awoke in very bad humor. His wife having left for France eight days ago, he was feeling disconsolate. Incredible though it seems, in all the ten years since their marriage, this is the first time that Mrs Edith Smith, the professional beauty, has been so long absent from home; two or three days usually suffice for her frequent trips to Europe. The first thing that Mr Smith does is to connect his phonotelephote, the wires of which communicate with his Paris mansion. The telephote! Here is another of the great triumphs of science in our time. The transmission of speech is an old story; the transmission of images by means of sensitive mirrors connected by wires is a thing but of yesterday. A valuable invention indeed, and Mr Smith this morning was not niggard of blessings for the inventor, when by its aid he was able distinctly to see his wife notwithstanding the distance that separated him from her. Mrs Smith, weary after the ball or the visit to the theater the preceding night, is still abed, though it is near noontide at Paris. She is asleep, her head sunk in the lace-covered pillows. What? She stirs? Her lips move. She is dreaming perhaps? Yes, dreaming. She is talking, pronouncing a name—his name—Fritz! The delightful vision gave a happier turn to Mr Smith's thoughts. And now, at the call of imperative duty, light–hearted he springs from his bed and enters his mechanical dresser.

Two minutes later the machine deposited him all dressed at the threshold of his office. The round of journalistic work was now begun. First he enters the hall of the novel–writers, a vast apartment crowned with an enormous transparent cupola. In one corner is a telephone, through which a hundred Earth Chronicle littérateurs in turn recount to the public in daily installments a hundred novels. Addressing one of these authors who was waiting his turn, 'Capital! Capital! my dear fellow,' said he, 'your last story. The scene where the village maid discusses interesting philosophical problems with her lover shows your very acute power of observation. Never have the ways of country folk been better portrayed. Keep on, my dear Archibald, keep on! Since yesterday, thanks to you, there is a gain of 5000 subscribers.'

'Mr John Last,' he began again, turning to a new arrival, 'I am not so well pleased with your work. Your story is not a picture of life; it lacks the elements of truth. And why? Simply because you run straight on to the end; because you do not analyze. Your heroes do this thing or that from this or that motive, which you assign without ever a thought of dissecting their mental and moral natures. Our feelings, you must remember, are far more complex than all that. In real life every act is the resultant of a hundred thoughts that come and go, and these you must study, each by itself, if you would create a living character. 'But,' you will say, 'in order to note these fleeting thoughts one must know them, must be able to follow them in their capricious meanderings.' Why, any child can do that, as you know. You have simply to make use of hypnotism, electrical or human, which gives one a two–fold being, setting free the witness–personality so that it may see, understand, and remember the reasons which determine the personality that acts. Just study yourself as you live from day to day, my dear Last. Imitate your associate whom I was complimenting a moment ago. Let yourself be hypnotized. What's that? You have tried it already? Not sufficiently, then, not sufficiently!'

Mr Smith continues his round and enters the reporters' hall. Here 1500 reporters, in their respective places, facing an equal number of telephones, are communicating to the subscribers the news of the world as gathered during the night. The organization of this matchless service has often been described. Besides his telephone, each reporter, as the reader is aware, has in front of him a set of commutators, which enable him to communicate with any desired telephotic line. Thus the subscribers not only hear the news but see the occurrences. When an incident is described that is already past, photographs of its main features are transmitted with the narrative. And there is no confusion withal. The reporters' items, just like the different stories and all the other component parts of the journal, are classified automatically according to an ingenious system, and reach the hearer in due succession. Furthermore, the hearers are free to listen only to what specially concerns them. They may at pleasure give attention to one editor and refuse it to another.

Mr Smith next addresses one of the ten reporters in the astronomical department—a department still in the embryonic stage, but which will yet play an important part in journalism.

'Well, Cash, what's the news?'

'We have phototelegrams from Mercury, Venus, and Mars.'

'Are those from Mars of any interest?'

'Yes, indeed. There is a revolution in the Central Empire.'

'And what of Jupiter?' asked Mr Smith.

'Nothing as yet. We cannot quite understand their signals. Perhaps ours do not reach them.'

'That's bad,' exclaimed Mr Smith, as he hurried away, not in the best of humor, toward the hall of the scientific editors. With their heads bent down over their electric computers, thirty scientific men were absorbed in transcendental calculations. The coming of Mr Smith was like the falling of a bomb among them.

'Well, gentlemen, what is this I hear? No answer from Jupiter? Is it always to be thus? Come, Cooley, you have been at work now twenty years on this problem, and yet—'

'True enough,' replied the man addressed. 'Our science of optics is still very defective, and through our mile–and–three–quarter telescopes—'

'Listen to that, Peer,' broke in Mr Smith, turning to a second scientist. 'Optical science defective! Optical science is your specialty. But,' he continued, again addressing William Cooley, 'failing with Jupiter, are we getting any results from the moon?'

'The case is no better there.'

'This time you do not lay the blame on the science of optics. The moon is immeasurably less distant than Mars, yet with Mars our communication is fully established. I presume you will not say that you lack telescopes?'

'Telescopes? O no, the trouble here is about—inhabitants!'

'That's it,' added Peer.

'So, then, the moon is positively uninhabited?' asked Mr Smith.

'At least,' answered Cooley, 'on the face which she presents to us. As for the opposite side, who knows?'

'Ah, the opposite side! You think, then,' remarked Mr Smith, musingly, 'that if one could but—'

'Could what?'

'Why, turn the moon about–face.'

'Ah, there's something in that,' cried the two men at once. And indeed, so confident was their air, they seemed to have no doubt as to the possibility of success in such an undertaking.

'Meanwhile,' asked Mr Smith, after a moment's silence, 'have you no news of interest today?'

'Indeed we have,' answered Cooley. 'The elements of Olympus are definitively settled. That great planet gravitates beyond Neptune at the mean distance of 11,400,799,642 miles from the sun, and to traverse its vast orbit takes 1311 years, 294 days, 12 hours, 43 minutes, 9 seconds.'

'Why didn't you tell me that sooner?' cried Mr Smith. 'Now inform the reporters of this straightway. You know how eager is the curiosity of the public with regard to these astronomical questions. That news must go into today's issue.'

Then, the two men bowing to him, Mr Smith passed into the next hall, an enormous gallery upward of 3200 feet in length, devoted to atmospheric advertising. Every one has noticed those enormous advertisements reflected from the clouds, so large that they may be seen by the populations of whole cities or even of entire countries. This, too, is one of Mr Fritz Napoleon Smith's ideas, and in the Earth Chronicle building a thousand projectors are constantly engaged in displaying upon the clouds these mammoth advertisements.

When Mr Smith today entered the sky–advertising department, he found the operators sitting with folded arms at their motionless projectors, and inquired as to the cause of their inaction. In response, the man addressed simply pointed to the sky, which was of a pure blue. 'Yes,' muttered Mr Smith, 'a cloudless sky! That's too bad, but what's to be done? Shall we produce rain? That we might do, but is it of any use? What we need is clouds, not rain. Go,' said he, addressing the head engineer, 'go see Mr Samuel Mark, of the meteorological division of the scientific department, and tell him for me to go to work in earnest on the question of artificial clouds. It will never do for us to be always thus at the mercy of cloudless skies!'

Mr Smith's daily tour through the several departments of his newspaper is now finished. Next, from the advertisement hall he passes to the reception chamber, where the ambassadors accredited to the American government are awaiting him, desirous of having a word of counsel or advice from the all–powerful editor. A discussion was going on when he entered. 'Your Excellency will pardon me,' the French Ambassador was saying to the Russian, 'but I see nothing in the map of Europe that requires change. 'The North for the Slavs?' Why, yes, of course; but the South for the Latins. Our common frontier, the Rhine, it seems to me, serves very well. Besides, my government, as you must know, will firmly oppose every movement, not only against Paris, our capital, or our two great prefectures, Rome and Madrid, but also against the kingdom of Jerusalem, the dominion of Saint Peter, of which France means to be the trusty defender.'

'Well said!' exclaimed Mr Smith. 'How is it,' he asked, turning to the Russian ambassador, 'that you Russians are not content with your vast empire, the most extensive in the world, stretching from the banks of the Rhine to the Celestial Mountains and the Kara-Korum, whose shores are washed by the Frozen Ocean, the Atlantic, the Mediterranean, and the Indian Ocean? Then, what is the use of threats? Is war possible in view of modern inventions—asphyxiating shells capable of being projected a distance of 60 miles, an electric spark of 90 miles, that can at one stroke annihilate a battalion; to say nothing of the plague, the cholera, the yellow fever, that the belligerents might spread among their antagonists mutually, and which would in a few days destroy the greatest armies?'

'True,' answered the Russian; 'but can we do all that we wish? As for us Russians, pressed on our eastern frontier by the Chinese, we must at any cost put forth our strength for an effort toward the west.'

'O, is that all? In that case,' said Mr Smith, 'the thing can be arranged. I will speak to the Secretary of State about it. The attention of the Chinese government shall be called to the matter. This is not the first time that the Chinese have bothered us.'

'Under these conditions, of course—' And the Russian ambassador declared himself satisfied.

'Ah, Sir John, what can I do for you?' asked Mr Smith as he turned to the representative of the people of Great Britain, who till now had remained silent.

'A great deal,' was the reply. 'If the Earth Chronicle would but open a campaign on our behalf—'

'And for what object?'

'Simply for the annulment of the Act of Congress annexing to the United States the British islands.'

Though, by a just turn–about of things here below, Great Britain has become a colony of the United States, the English are not yet reconciled to the situation. At regular intervals they are ever addressing to the American government vain complaints.

'A campaign against the annexation that has been an accomplished fact for 150 years!' exclaimed Mr Smith. 'How can your people suppose that I would do anything so unpatriotic?'

'We at home think that your people must now be sated. The Monroe doctrine is fully applied; the whole of America belongs to the Americans. What more do you want? Besides, we will pay for what we ask.'

'Indeed!' answered Mr Smith, without manifesting the slightest irritation. 'Well, you English will ever be the same. No, no, Sir John, do not count on me for help. Give up our fairest province, Britain? Why not ask France generously to renounce possession of Africa, that magnificent colony the complete conquest of which cost her the labor of 800 years? You will be well received!'

'You decline! All is over then!' murmured the British agent sadly. 'The United Kingdom falls to the share of the Americans; the Indies to that of—'

'The Russians,' said Mr Smith, completing the sentence.

'Australia—'

'Has an independent government.'

'Then nothing at all remains for us!' sighed Sir John, downcast.

'Nothing?' asked Mr Smith, laughing. 'Well, now, there's Gibraltar!'

With this sally the audience ended. The clock was striking twelve, the hour of breakfast. Mr Smith returns to his chamber. Where the bed stood in the morning a table all spread comes up through the floor. For Mr Smith, being above all a practical man, has reduced the problem of existence to its simplest terms. For him, instead of the endless suites of apartments of the olden time, one room fitted with ingenious mechanical contrivances is enough. Here he sleeps, takes his meals, in short, lives.

He seats himself. In the mirror of the phonotelephote is seen the same chamber at Paris which appeared in it this morning. A table furnished forth is likewise in readiness here, for notwithstanding the difference of hours, Mr Smith and his wife have arranged to take their meals simultaneously. It is delightful thus to take breakfast tête–à–tête with one who is 3000 miles or so away. Just now, Mrs Smith's chamber has no occupant.

'She is late! Woman's punctuality! Progress everywhere except there!' muttered Mr Smith as he turned the tap for the first dish. For like all wealthy folk in our day, Mr Smith has done away with the domestic kitchen and is a subscriber to the Grand Alimentation Company, which sends through a great network of tubes to subscribers' residences all sorts of dishes, as a varied assortment is always in readiness. A subscription costs money, to be sure, but the cuisine is of the best, and the system has this advantage, that it does away with the pestering race of the cordons–bleus. Mr Smith received and ate, all alone, the hors–d'oeuvre, entrées, rôti, and legumes that constituted the repast. He was just finishing the dessert when Mrs Smith appeared in the mirror of the telephote.

'Why, where have you been?' asked Mr Smith through the telephone.

'What! You are already at the dessert? Then I am late,' she exclaimed, with a winsome naïveté. 'Where have I been, you ask? Why, at my dress–maker's. The hats are just lovely this season! I suppose I forgot to note the time, and so am a little late.'

'Yes, a little,' growled Mr Smith; 'so little that I have already quite finished breakfast. Excuse me if I leave you now, but I must be going.'

'O certainly, my dear; good–by till evening.'

Smith stepped into his air–coach, which was in waiting for him at a window. 'Where do you wish to go, sir?' inquired the coachman.

'Let me see; I have three hours,' Mr Smith mused.

'Jack, take me to my accumulator works at Niagara.'

For Mr Smith has obtained a lease of the great falls of Niagara. For ages the energy developed by the falls went unutilized. Smith, applying Jackson's invention, now collects this energy, and lets or sells it. His visit to the works took more time than he had anticipated. It was four o'clock when he returned home, just in time for the daily audience which he grants to callers.

One readily understands how a man situated as Smith is must be beset with requests of all kinds. Now it is an inventor needing capital; again it is some visionary who comes to advocate a brilliant scheme which must surely yield millions of profit. A choice has to be made between these projects, rejecting the worthless, examining the questionable ones, accepting the meritorious. To this work Mr Smith devotes every day two full hours.

The callers were fewer today than usual—only twelve of them. Of these, eight had only impracticable schemes to propose. In fact, one of them wanted to revive painting, an art fallen into desuetude owing to the progress made in color–photography. Another, a physician, boasted that he had discovered a cure for nasal catarrh! These impracticables were dismissed in short order. Of the four projects favorably received, the first was that of a young man whose broad forehead betokened his intellectual power.

'Sir, I am a chemist,' he began, 'and as such I come to you.'

'Well!'

'Once the elementary bodies,' said the young chemist, 'were held to be sixty-two in number; a hundred years ago they were reduced to ten; now only three remain irresolvable, as you are aware.'

'Yes, yes.'

'Well, sir, these also I will show to be composite. In a few months, a few weeks, I shall have succeeded in solving the problem. Indeed, it may take only a few days.'

'And then?'

'Then, sir, I shall simply have determined the absolute. All I want is money enough to carry my research to a successful issue.'

'Very well,' said Mr Smith. 'And what will be the practical outcome of your discovery?'

'The practical outcome? Why, that we shall be able to produce easily all bodies whatever—stone, wood, metal, fibers—'

'And flesh and blood?' queried Mr Smith, interrupting him. 'Do you pretend that you expect to manufacture a human being out and out?'

'Why not?'

Mr Smith advanced $100,000 to the young chemist, and engaged his services for the Earth Chronicle laboratory.

The second of the four successful applicants, starting from experiments made so long ago as the nineteenth century and again and again repeated, had conceived the idea of removing an entire city all at once from one place to another. His special project had to do with the city of Granton, situated, as everybody knows, some fifteen miles inland. He proposes to transport the city on rails and to change it into a watering–place. The profit, of course, would be enormous. Mr Smith, captivated by the scheme, bought a half–interest in it.

'As you are aware, sir,' began applicant No. 3, 'by

the aid of our solar and terrestrial accumulators and transformers, we are able to make all the seasons the same. I propose to do something better still. Transform into heat a portion of the surplus energy at our disposal; send this heat to the poles; then the polar regions, relieved of their snow–cap, will become a vast territory available for man's use. What think you of the scheme?'

'Leave your plans with me, and come back in a week. I will have them examined in the meantime.'

Finally, the fourth announced the early solution of a weighty scientific problem. Every one will remember the bold experiment made a hundred years ago by Dr Nathaniel Faithburn. The doctor, being a firm believer in human hibernation—in other words, in the possibility of our suspending our vital functions and of calling them into action again after a time—resolved to subject the theory to a practical test. To this end, having first made his last will and pointed out the proper method of awakening him; having also directed that his sleep was to continue a hundred years to a day from the date of his apparent death, he unhesitatingly put the theory to the proof in his own person. Reduced to the condition of a mummy, Dr Faithburn was coffined and laid in a tomb. Time went on. September 25th, 2889, being the day set for his resurrection, it was proposed to Mr Smith that he should permit the second part of the experiment to be performed at his residence this evening.

'Agreed. Be here at ten o'clock,' answered Mr Smith; and with that the day's audience was closed.

Left to himself, feeling tired, he lay down on an extension chair. Then, touching a knob, he established communication with the Central Concert Hall, whence our greatest maestros send out to subscribers their delightful successions of accords determined by recondite algebraic formulas. Night was approaching. Entranced by the harmony, forgetful of the hour, Smith did not notice that it was growing dark. It was quite dark when he was aroused by the sound of a door opening. 'Who is there?' he asked, touching a commutator.

Suddenly, in consequence of the vibrations produced, the air became luminous.

'Ah! you, Doctor?'

'Yes,' was the reply. 'How are you?'

'I am feeling well.'

'Good! Let me see your tongue. All right! Your pulse. Regular! And your appetite?'

'Only passably good.'

'Yes, the stomach. There's the rub. You are over–worked. If your stomach is out of repair, it must be mended. That requires study. We must think about it.'

'In the meantime,' said Mr Smith, 'you will dine with me.'

As in the morning, the table rose out of the floor. Again, as in the morning, the potage, rôti, ragoûts, and legumes were supplied through the food–pipes. Toward the close of the meal, phonotelephotic communication was made with Paris. Smith saw his wife, seated alone at the dinner–table, looking anything but pleased at her loneliness.

'Pardon me, my dear, for having left you alone,' he said through the telephone. 'I was with Dr Wilkins.'

'Ah, the good doctor!' remarked Mrs Smith, her countenance lighting up.

'Yes. But, pray, when are you coming home?'

'This evening.'

'Very well. Do you come by tube or by air–train?'

'Oh, by tube.'

'Yes; and at what hour will you arrive?'

'About eleven, I suppose.'

'Eleven by Centropolis time, you mean?'

'Yes.'

'Good–by, then, for a little while,' said Mr Smith as he severed communication with Paris.

Dinner over, Dr Wilkins wished to depart. 'I shall expect you at ten,' said Mr Smith. 'Today, it seems, is the day for the return to life of the famous Dr Faithburn. You did not think of it, I suppose. The awakening is to take place here in my house. You must come and see. I shall depend on your being here.'

'I will come back,' answered Dr Wilkins.

Left alone, Mr Smith busied himself with examining

his accounts—a task of vast magnitude, having to do with transactions which involve a daily expenditure of upward of $800,000. Fortunately, indeed, the stupendous progress of mechanic art in modern times makes it comparatively easy. Thanks to the Piano Electro–Reckoner, the most complex calculations can be made in a few seconds. In two hours Mr Smith completed his task. Just in time. Scarcely had he turned over the last page when Dr Wilkins arrived. After him came the body of Dr Faithburn, escorted by a numerous company of men of science. They commenced work at once. The casket being laid down in the middle of the room, the telephote was got in readiness. The outer world, already notified, was anxiously expectant, for the whole world could be eye–witnesses of the performance, a reporter meanwhile, like the chorus in the ancient drama, explaining it all viva voce through the telephone.

'They are opening the casket,' he explained. 'Now they are taking Faithburn out of it—a veritable mummy, yellow, hard, and dry. Strike the body and it resounds like a block of wood. They are now applying heat; now electricity. No result. These experiments are suspended for a moment while Dr Wilkins makes an examination of the body. Dr Wilkins, rising, declares the man to be dead. 'Dead!' exclaims every one present. 'Yes,' answers Dr Wilkins, 'dead!' 'And how long has he been dead?' Dr Wilkins makes another examination. 'A hundred years,' he replies.'

The case stood just as the reporter said. Faithburn was

dead, quite certainly dead! 'Here is a method that needs improvement,' remarked Mr Smith to Dr Wilkins, as the scientific committee on hibernation bore the casket out. 'So much for that experiment. But if poor Faithburn is dead, at least he is sleeping,' he continued. 'I wish I could get some sleep. I am tired out, Doctor, quite tired out! Do you not think that a bath would refresh me?'

'Certainly. But you must wrap yourself up well before you go out into the hall–way. You must not expose yourself to cold.'

'Hall–way? Why, Doctor, as you well know, everything is done by machinery here. It is not for me to go to the bath; the bath will come to me. Just look!' and he pressed a button. After a few seconds a faint rumbling was heard, which grew louder and louder. Suddenly the door opened, and the tub appeared.

Such, for this year of grace 2889, is the history of one day in the life of the editor of the Earth Chronicle. And the history of that one day is the history of 365 days every year, except leap–years, and then of 366 days—for as yet no means has been found of increasing the length of the terrestrial year.